MYTHIC

Also by Mike Allen

DEFACING THE MOON
PETTING THE TIME SHARK
DISTURBING MUSES
STRANGE WISDOMS OF THE DEAD

As editor:

NEW DOMINIONS:
FANTASY STORIES BY VIRGINIA WRITERS

THE ALCHEMY OF STARS:
RHYSLING AWARD WINNERS SHOWCASE
(with Roger Dutcher)

MYTHIC

edited by
Mike Allen

Mythic
Delirium
Books

MYTHIC

Published by Mythic Delirium Books
http://www.mythicdelirium.com
in cooperation with Prime Books
http://www.prime-books.com

ACKNOWLEDGMENTS: My gratitude, to Sean Wallace,
who provided me with the idea, the strategy and the
tools; to Anita Allen, for her support, advice and
insight; to Sonya Taaffe, for her suggestions and
enthusiasm; to all the contributors, for their willing-
ness to join me in the leap.
— *Mike Allen, March 2006*

Contents

Vandana Singh
Syllables of Old Lore

I will speak, if I must
Through patterns drawn in the dust
Through the wind, whispering syllables
Of old lore to the leaves
I will speak like clouds
In the sunset, edged with rust
Gathered like coils of tresses
Across the face of the sky
My words are ash on the lips
They shrivel on the tongue
Returning to the womb
Of silence. So I must speak slant
In languages I can trust
Wind, leaves, clouds and rain
A symbolic tongue of joy and pain
Words caught a while in time and space
Returning then to dust, to dust.

Sonya Taaffe
Exorcisms

THIS IS THE INSIDE of a woman's head. This is looking out through her eyes that are like the eyes of a mask, bone frames and curtains of skin; she blinks and inside her head, seeded close behind her eyes, the spirit curls like the unborn she once was. The woman sips coffee, and the spirit tastes on their shared tongue the rich, burnt bitterness of a drink she never knew when alive. They drank tea, where she lived: in glasses, and you could hold sugar on your tongue while you sipped.

The spirit shifts, finds a roomier resting place in the crannies of thought between how to hold a pencil and first fumbled words, observes the woman's hand penciling letters across a page: quick sharp down-strokes, absurd jaunty tails on "g" and "y" dashed away back-pointing to the left where the letters incline; a backwards progression, to her eyes. Left to right, the wrong way across the page. But she has grown accustomed to the idea, this spirit that tucks herself around a memory of kisses in spring rain; she reads now, through others' eyes, the languages of more lands than she ever saw in her life. Then she saw one country, and one town of it, and the uneasy circling of the world outside: the bells that rang the orthodox hours, you could hear them when the wind blew crosswise Sunday mornings. Soft smoke of prayer and incense, frightened she could smell it drifting in the dusty streets; her own day of rest flavored with the scents of fresh bread broken and wax slipping down the side of a burning candle, its dip and flicker the light that dances from the bride's bright raiment when she enters at sunset and you greet her with song: she still knows all the words. If she sang them with this woman's mouth, who would hear her?

She came over the sea in the skull of the student she loved, fitted between seventy-two letters like flicks of black flame and a shadow-sketch of the demon who comes to young men by night, rouses them in their sleep and sucks out their lives with their seed; all her daughters are like her and she breeds them from the young men she milks. At nights, the student tossed in dreams half delicious, half nightmare, never knowing who he really carried in the curves of his brain. Because he had sworn himself to her forever, when they clasped living hands in the shadow of her uncle's house and did not dare kiss, she lived within him until he died: young, of a fever, in a sweating tenement in summer. He had less than fifty words in this city's language and one of them was his name, such as it had survived immigration. By the time she parted from his ebbing spirit, cajoling it to join her, knowing it never would, she could mourn him in the tongue of the land he had chosen, golden land, paved with stone and filthy brick. Opportunity killed him, freed her. She took up residence below the memories of his sister, who had come ahead with her lover until they turned him away at the gates — his health, he was never strong; strong enough to cross wheat fields and mountains and an ocean that almost heaved out his stomach but not to step through a doorway? — and swam in the woman's dreams of her dead brother already transformed into a saint, one of the thirty-six on whose back the world rests, sweet and sanctified and studying now in the company of the great sages of the past. Together, they shed tears. In their joined mouth, syllables of the language older than what they spoke when they spoke to God, speaking to God now, speaking life. On the mourning woman's lips, a smile she did not feel: inside her head, the hopeless laughter of a soul that will never die.

Now, undying, nor dead, she makes a restless circuit of this woman's thoughts. Three generations have come and gone since that first girl covered the mirrors for her brother; this one bears the name of the student's sister, this woman who is writing, by pencil and paper, anachronistic as the teardrop shape of stubborn life that swarms her veins, a history of her family as well as she knows it. Lashes sweep down, fence out light, lift permitting the spirit to crowd against the concave of dark irises and gaze down at the page. So many things, wrong. We never spelled our name that way. The town had another name. The border shifted; sometimes it was there, sometimes elsewhere, who kept track? Yes, he said that. No, she did not. What scraps and patches have lasted down to this time? She is a scrap herself, thought-blown in the remembrances of another. Rags like her great-grandfather sold on another century's streets.

The hand moves on, inscribing fact tattered into fiction: there, there, the woman hears a murmur of pain and recognition breathe from her lips, like seeing the face of a long-lost love before they wash him for the grave, like touching the stone of your house fire-blackened and forgotten, there the spirit sees the name of a girl this woman's ancestor loved, a family legend, whose heart broke when he could not marry her, whose spirit, they swore, possessed him so that he would speak in a voice not his own and say things the gentle student would never think, almost they called a wonder-worker to exorcise their son but the spirit subsided, the possession was over, he left for America in the best of health to find his sister and her lover; the first he found, the second he never saw again, the third rode softly in his dreams until the final fever vision consumed him and she lost him forever.

Still they are twined, like candle-wicks, like the sweet braid of Shabbos bread: remembered inseparable, impossibly rejoined. The lines of his palm that only she remembers, life, love, heart stopped and broken; woven with her own, on finer paper than ever he could afford. And she is weeping, as she has not wept since she keened Kaddish in another woman's voice; someone else's tears smear and spot the neat eccentric hand and when she wipes them away, graphite blurs out the name of the beloved, the ghost, what cleaves to her even now.

She blurs away, like their names made a smoke-cloud on the white paper hatched with blue, the letters that comprise her being run away into nothing like the old story; though she does not wear a holy name on her forehead, she wears her own name in her heart, and his. Together they bound her to the world he left long ago: now she cannot help but follow. Into light, into darkness, into Gehenna, into Paradise, she cleaves to him as once she clung to his memory in the blood of his sister. She is going, now. The other side of the grave is the other side of a mirror. The way that demons go: she is not a demon anymore, she never was, though when he dreamed of Lilith he dreamed her face. What does a reflection look like from the other side? She passes through the mirror and is gone.

This is the inside of a woman's head. This is looking out through her eyes, which are nothing more than eyes now, they slide to the page and back, they blink, they are filling with tears that she cannot explain: someone is dead and she is weeping for joy. She lifts her pencil, bends to write again. Here, the grandfather; here, the textiles; here, the poetry; where one unravels another begins. A shame that no one knows how family stories end.

Lawrence Schimel
Kristallnacht

She wore glass spectacles
for her vision was clouded,
as if that night her family's home
was burned to the ground in a pogrom
the smoke had gotten into her eyes
and never left them.

They named her Cinderella
when they pulled her from the ashes,
their hearts going soft because
she was only three years old.
Years later, her stepsisters teased
that she was named Cinderella
because she was dark as soot.
They pinched her bold nose
and pulled her black hair
and powdered their pale faces
to go to parties with the Viennese elite.

Cinderella, of course, was never invited
to attend these lavish social functions;
her foster family happily left her at home,
working while they danced, dreaming
of the day she was asked to accompany them.
She was always certain it would not be long,
and therefore worked unfailingly, hoping
for approval.

While her stepsisters primped and prepped
to waltz among princes, Cinderella walked
to the market, stepping over sewage in the gutters,
dodging the nimble rats that boldly crossed
the streets in search of food. A kindly frau
who sat beside a cart of squash — yellow gourds
and fat pumpkins like lumpy little suns —
    stopped her.
She took Cinderella's hands into her own.
"You look so sad, dear. I will help you."
The woman drew Cinderella into the shadows
of the alleyway, and pulled papers from her pocket.
"Take these," she said. "They are mine,
but I am old. Go to America instead of me.
Find a new life. Send for your family,
if any are still alive. I am too old to begin again.
But for you, there is still hope for you."

Cinderella stared at this woman. "I am
no Jew," she said, handing back the papers.
She walked away, but the frau's words —
the insinuations, the generosity —
haunted her. She walked faster,
trying to outrun the echoes in her mind.

Passing a shop window, Cinderella saw
a pair of slippers made of glass.
If she had been invited to the ball,
she thought, she would love to wear
those slippers. She stared at them,
longing, and her reflection stared back:
swart, square. Semitic.

She bought the slippers with the grocery money
and hurried back to the now-empty house.
Cinderella powdered her face
with the stepsisters' cosmetics,
put on one of their dresses.
She tied her dark hair in a knot and hid it
beneath a silver scarf. But still her nose betrayed her.
She didn't care. She slipped on her glass shoes
and made her way across town to the gala event,
dreaming of finding a prince who would love her
and adore her and take her away to an enchanted life
where it did not matter that she looked like a Jew.

The party was as dazzling as she had always
        dreamed.
No one stopped her at the door, or paid her any
notice at all, it seemed, though some people stared
at her. No one spoke to her. And then a shriek
made Cinderella the center of attention,
as her two stepsisters ran toward her.
"You are not fit to be seen here!" they cried.
They snatched the spectacles from her face
and, in front of the assembled crowd,
crushed them underfoot with a delicate
twist of the toe, grinding downward.

Cinderella's vision blurred without her glasses.
Tears burned in her eyes. And then suddenly,
the smoke that had clouded her sight
for as long as she could recall
lifted. She saw, at last, what she had always

overlooked before: these people had killed
her family, had meant to kill her as well.

She stood there, numb, as the stepsisters
poked and pushed her. They stepped
on her toes and broke her glass slippers
into hundreds of sharp splinters.

Cinderella left the shards of her glass shoes
on the dance floor and walked barefoot
out of the hall, leaving footprints of blood
behind her. She was never seen again.

Matthew Cheney
In Exile

WHEN BLIN WAS BORN I dreamed of the sea, because so many of the stories my own mother told me in my young years described an endless sea, and the endless sea brought heroes home. I dreamed of depths and monsters, of fish the size of houses, of houses in the caves at the bottom of the blue of the sea. I imagined Lake Tenebro (where I swam each day in the warm winters of home) deeper and deeper than ever it had been: that was all I could imagine of the sea. Now that I can stand every morning with waves scattering themselves toward my feet, I wonder at how easily the truth overtook all that I imagined for so many years — overtook it with such force that I have trouble remembering what I once imagined, and to remember Lake Tenebro now I must think of the sea being captured, contained, hollowed out until it is a shallow, quiet place where children swim each morning during warm winters.

The wind picks up again, and I huddle into my coat. I can see the silhouettes of far-off villagers, and I know they will need me soon to help haul in the mermaids' catch, the bulging nets of seaweed and squid and drowned sailors, the treasure that we drag like a rippling whale over the beach and bring to the sorters, cutters, weighers, gutters, salters, traders, priests, and cooks.

It is a cold, damp life here, and I hate the sea.

* * *

TELL ME, LUSHAN, is it because of you that I am here? Because you burned down Ursula's house in your rage at me? Because after years of war you did not like the peace you returned to? Because you wanted Blin to watch his mother run off through the forest at night?

Should I give you that power, Lushan? The power to determine for me why I fled? My melancholy makes me yearn to pass whatever choices I have made over to other forces; a pitiful, perhaps pitiable, condition. I write to you now on pressed mermaid scales with ink from a squid (common things here, though they still feel exotic to me). Are there travelers to take this letter for me? Will I let them take it?

It took me — assuming my count is correct — almost six months to cross to the coast, and then longer still to wander from one sad little settlement to another until I came to the village here, a place some people call a city, though it is smaller than the smallest borough of our smallest city. We do not do well, our people, near the sea.

I have wanted to tell you so much. I have seen so much, and I want to discover words for it all. I want you to think of me, and I want you to tell Blin stories about me, because I don't want him to forget that I —

(No, I will not send this letter to you.)

I REFLECT:

During the wars, I planted gardens. They surrounded our little house, the brightest flowers set to receive morning sun near the front door, the plants that provided most of our food set where the after-noon sun drifted through the tops of the forest's trees at the back of the house. The plants grew and grew until they were as tall as I, then taller, their stalks thick and green, each petal of the flowers larger than my hands. The house was hidden by the garden, and the neighbors laughed when they passed by. "Does Amimone hide in her garden?" they said between their chuckles. "Have the flowers devoured her?"

One time, a child came to the garden, one of the children from the far end of town, the son of a family I did not know. At first I thought he was a girl, but he was not. He tried to climb a fireflower, and seemed surprised when it bent under his weight. He screamed as he drifted to the ground. "Make it go faster!" he said when I came running. He climbed up again, and this time the stalk broke and he fell to the soft dirt, the yellow flowers scattering around him. "Was that better?" I asked. "Yes!" he said. "Please don't do it again," I said, adding: "I like the flowers and don't want them all to fall to the ground." He cackled and ran off into the forest.

I wish I had asked his name, because I'm sure that within a year or two he was called to the wars. All the men were, and even some of the stronger women or the ones without children, and the children themselves once they were ten years old, and I'm sure the boy who visited my garden was nearly ten. Every morning the old crier would wander through the streets, hollering the names of the next to go. At night, sometimes, she would go through the streets more slowly and call out more quietly the names of the known dead, and the names would whisper down the streets and through the cracks in doors and windows and walls.

Until the day when the crier ran through the city, calling out the end of the wars. The news removed decades from her, and when she stopped running, she stood tall, her eyes bright, her grey hair glistening as if it were gold. The evil one had been destroyed, she yelled out toward the houses and the sky. His lands were ruined, his armies slaughtered, his slaves freed, the awful darkness of the past eons lifted. A week later, our soldiers returned, battered and battle-scarred but emboldened, radiating victorious fury. They tromped through the streets, cracking the paving stones with their heavy boots, they trampled the commons with revelry, they emptied the pubs of every last bit of ale, they ravaged wives and daughters and husbands and sons in desperate lust. I saw Lushan when his brigade tumbled through the city gates, but though his face was familiar the inferno in his eyes frightened me, and I turned away and ran home and locked the door, holding Blin in my arms as if he were still the infant he had been when his father went away. We stayed huddled together until Lushan and a gang of fellow soldiers stumbled toward the house, screaming and calling to every god and demon whose name they could remember. They slashed my flowers with their swords, dug in the dirt with their boots, splattered fruits and vegetables over their heads and under their feet, laughing the whole time, hollering, pounding on the walls and the locked door. "Come out, wife!" Lushan called through the window.

"Come and see your husband's victory!" He stood back so I could watch as he lowered his pants and held himself, engorged, and then the widow of his old friend Mot, drunk and half-naked, her breasts drooping from her tattered blouse, knelt down beside him and brought him to a climax as the other men cheered her on.

In the morning, they all lay like puppies in the yard, their clothes dampened by dew and piss and vomit. I unlocked the door and brought them water one-by-one, saving Lushan for last. "I dreamed you had a beautiful garden," he said. Tears dripped down his face as he embraced me. I wrapped my arms around him, but I did not hold him tight.

AFTER THE HARVEST and the feast and the apportioning, I brought the scraps that were given to me (the newcomer, the stranger, the alien) back to the hut I call my house, and I inventoried my belongings. I developed this habit soon after I left the city, because who can tell what disappears in the night unless they know exactly what they have before sleep?

Tonight I have my cloak, one dress that is frayed but still elegant, a heavy shirt and heavy pants for working, two sets of underwear, a sweater, two pairs of socks, leather boots with their soles recently repaired by an old and raving cordwainer I met along the shore, a red blanket, a bone knife, a canvas satchel, a whale-oil lantern, some bits of flint, a wooden mug, a metal plate, a fork I whittled from a tree branch, Blin's favorite doll, four quills I made from the feathers of a gull, a pile of pressed scales, and a bladder of ink. I add tonight's acquisitions: a batch of seaweed, a belt from a drowned man, a rusty telescope from a sunken ship, and a new bladder of ink.

My eyes and skin sting from the salt blown in off the sea. I sit on a bit of driftwood beside the little fire that warms the hut, my house, and wish I knew where to find a tea kettle and some tea. Tonight that is what I miss the most: a hot cup of tea held in my hands, the steam warming my face as my lips touch the edge of the cup.

I REFLECT:

At the time my friendship with Ursula deepened, I was living a happy life, raising Blin by myself, tending my garden, walking to the center of the city once a week to buy or sell or gossip. I worried about Lushan, who had been at the wars for more than a year by that time, but I no longer dreamed of him, my body no longer ached for his, my thoughts were not all prefaced by What would Lushan do — What would Lushan think — What would Lushan say . . . .

I had known Ursula my entire life, of course. We were born a month and three houses apart. But she spent most of her time farming the commons, while I was part of a family of woodworkers. After Lushan went to the wars, though, I began to rely on Ursula, who had become a healer and who sold better herbs and remedies than the dealers in the center of the city. I was scared of her at first, this tall, hawk-faced woman with long grey hair and a voice that sang bawdy songs at night, loud and lovely, shimmering through the trees. I bought my herbs and thanked her quietly every time until one day she said, "I might as well be a golem, it seems."

"What?" I said, shocked that she had said anything to me other than the price of what I wanted to buy.

"Have I done something to offend you?"

"Offend? No," I said.

"Then why don't you talk to me?"

"What should we — would you — do you want to talk about?"

"Tell me your favorite song."

"'Lorelei of the Springs,'" I said. It was not my favorite song, but it was the only title that came to me.

"I don't know that one very well," Ursula said. "Do you?"

"I know a bit of it."

"Then hum it for me."

"Hum?"

"Unless you want to sing it?" Ursula said.

"No no. I don't think I remember. Much of it. The song."

"Try humming it."

"I don't think — "

"Try."

And so I did. And not too badly, if I do say so. Only a few wrong notes here and there.

"Ahhh, yes yes yes!" Ursula said. And then she sang:

Bright Lorelei,
Drowning in the spring,
Couldn't someone bother to save her?
Dear Lorelei,
This song that we sing,
The only thing history gave her . . .

"Those aren't the words, are they?" Ursula said.

"No, I don't think so."

"Well, they should be." Indeed, I have remembered them ever since that day.

I HAVE THOUGHT RECENTLY of Pin and Pem, the youngsters who, shortly after the wars ended, decided everything needed to be stirred up again, and so they went to the village of men over on the borders of the Rathgeel mountains and dropped as many insults and insinuations as they could think of. They had been good children, twin brother and sister, and their parents were hardworking masons, their father one of the few who had not gone off to the war, his skills determined by the city council to be too valuable at home — his primary job in those years was to maintain the city's walls — and I remember seeing Pin and Pem out helping their parents many days, cutting stones or slathering mortar or pushing a wheelbarrow. But after the wars ended and the soldiers returned home, life became more chaotic. The pubs were busy at all hours, thieves and vagabonds haunted the night, the whores returned to Bethelsgate Bridge, and one night a group of revelers tried to set off fireworks and managed only to blow off somebody's arm and blast a head-sized hole in the city's south wall. Two days later, Pin and Pem set out.

We don't know, of course, what they said in the village of men, only what they said they said. Ursula heard the tale from one of her customers, who worked for the city council and overheard the interrogation. Again and again, Pin and Pem said, "We told them terrible things, the worst we could think of." The interrogators asked, "What did you say?" Pin and Pem said, "Terrible things." "Such as?" "Terrible things."

The result? "They laughed at us and told us to go home to our mummies and daddies, or they'd send us off to the desert lands. We told them terrible things, threatened them something awful, and they just laughed and said there's nothing we could do or say to make them do anything but laugh. And then they told us to stop wasting their time."

Wasting their time, indeed. The wars had been good to those men. They traded in every item imaginable, and taxed the major roads through the Rathgeels, the only roads that led to the rich lands, the last battles of the wars having ravaged everything to the west.

Many people did not believe Pin and Pem's story. They said the twins had run away because their father did awful things to them at night, or their mother was a madwoman, but, these gossips and gobblers said, the world beyond our city was too terrible, too frightening and lonely and ruined, the village of men too ghastly even to speak of, and so the twins returned, because an awful father or a mad mother is easier to bear than the plains where dead voices sing from empty cisterns and exhausted wells, grass grows black around informal graves, and smoldering dirt sends strands of smoke to the violet sky.

I STILL THINK OF YOU, Lushan, as I write this. It is not a letter, no, because I will not send it. You will not ever see it. I will destroy these words as soon as I am done with them. But they must live for a moment, and the thought of you gives them life for me.

You did not think I was sympathetic to all you had seen. Day after day you sat in the house, drinking ale until you collapsed. I cleaned up the vomit and the spilled and broken bottles, I washed the piss from your clothes, I carried you to bed, I let you grope and fondle, I bore the puke-stained kisses and the fumbling thrusts as you tried to enter me before you collapsed into yet another oblivion. You had been noble — I knew because you told me so yourself, and on the days when your friends came to call, before they all gave up on you, they told me too about your gallant deeds and courage, while I covered my bruises and limped to get them all more food, more drinks. By the end of the year your belly hung like a sack from your shirt and you wheezed when you hauled yourself up from the chair.

I began to look forward to the nights when Mot's widow, Elaine, showed up in the shadows at the edge of our yard. I listened at the window to your grunts and sighs, to her moans. I heard her ask you to live with her and love her, I heard your cruelty to her, your silence. "Bring her inside," I told you one night, and you did. I watched as you pushed her to the floor and tore her clothes off as she shrieked and screamed, horrified, and you smothered her with yourself. That is what it is to love him, I thought. Now you know, I thought. Should I have been more kind? Should I have shown sympathy, should I have pled with you and begged you and torn you from her? Perhaps. Instead, I watched, and then, as you seemed to be finishing, as blood from her mouth stained the floor, I went to Blin's room and picked him up — he, who had learned not to sob for fear of your slap — and carried him through the dark streets until, finally, we reached Ursula's house.

LATER:

As I ran through the dancing shadows cast by the flames of the burning house, Lushan's tormented face hovered in my eyes, a silent raging ghost my memory was powerless to kill. As I ran, the shadows dissipated into darkness and the meadow I ran through rose into forest, a dungeon of trees and undergrowth and impenetrable black night. My eyes stung with smoke, my lungs were tight, aching, and my legs shivered terribly, forcing me finally to fall to my knees on the damp forest floor like a resting marionette.

The ghostly image of Lushan's anger gave way to the darkness, but a voice took its place, a voice that mixed my own with his, saying: What have you done? You left your child and your lover in the flames, you ran from it all, from your child and your lover and your husband, you ran into the forest to hide in the shadows and die in the damp darkness, you will be remembered as the woman who destroyed everything she touched, you will be a legend for children to curse with rhymes and jeers, you cannot return, you cannot turn back, you cannot correct what you have done, you you you —

My eyes adjusted to the darkness and though my head was heavy, I looked up and saw in between the far-off tops of trees a shard of an orange moon, smokey clouds brushing across it. I stood, and began to walk through the forest and toward the sea.

THERE WAS TIME, though, between the night I fled to Ursula's house and the night I fled to the forest. There were entire days of anxious happiness.

"HAVE I DONE something to offend you?"

"Offend? No."

"Then why don't you talk to me?"

I could have fled then. I could have chuckled and smiled and said my thank yous and walked out into the misty rain that fell that day, walked out and not turned back, perhaps not ever returned — there are, after all, other healers, other sources of herbs. I could have hid in the house and tended my garden and raised my son and waited for my husband to return from the wars.

Instead, I stayed, I spoke, I hummed. (Those aren't the words, are they? No, I don't think so. Well, they should be.) When I walked out into the grey day, I was smiling. I returned the next day, even though I didn't need any herbs. I needed conversation, incidental chatter, nothing to be remembered, nothing to take seriously, nothing but a light tune to decorate the emotions rising toward the words. Distraction, amusement, company. Ursula helped me with the garden, and she helped me with Blin, and she helped me with the house — until one day we found ourselves spending the nights together as well as the days, and our lives entwined, and we were our own sort of family.

None of that is anything I should blame myself for. No, I do not have anything to answer for until the night Lushan kicked through the door of Ursula's house and threw her against the wall, then grabbed the little shovel beside the fireplace and spread hot coals throughout the house. As the flames crawled up the walls, up the curtains, toward the thatched roof, Blin screamed, Ursula picked him up and carried him outside, and Lushan faced me, the fire-filled shovel in his hand.

AN OLD WOMAN who says her name is Faith comes to visit me. She brings whale meat and cooks it over the fire for me.

I tell her she does not need to cook my food.

She asks if I am offended. I tell her no. She says she is well known for her cooking, and she is pleased to cook for someone. She saw me during the apportioning, and she was shamed by the behavior of the villagers. They don't understand, she says. Understand what? I ask her. That if we do not take care of each other, we will all die alone, she says. Faith says she does not want to die alone.

We eat together and tell stories. When we begin, the stories I tell are not true ones — I tell her my husband and son were killed in the wars, that the city I lived in was destroyed in a battle, that I was the only survivor. Her eyes fill with tears as my story becomes more and more vivid, as I lose not only my son and my husband but my parents and my siblings and my aunts and uncles and everyone I ever knew. I describe the dragon fires that consumed the city, melting the immense stone buildings that were so large they nearly touched the sky. The air filled with the smell of death, I say. The smell of burning. I tell her that I wandered for weeks and months, and here my story begins to resemble the truth, because my imagination is tired and I am ashamed of myself for lying to an old woman. I tell her about the kindness of the people who brought me food or gave me a blanket or clothes, about the fear that filled me when I slept outside at night and heard bandits in the forest, heard people screaming as they were robbed and tortured and killed. I don't tell her that there were many days when I tried to return home, but discovered I had lost my way, that the only sure direction was the direction leading to the sea.

She says she once lived in a place far from here. She was a young woman, and her husband was injured in a duel — he fought for her honor, she said. But he died within a year of being wounded. She was afraid of the other man, the man who fought her husband, and so she joined a band of players and journeyed from town to town as the cook to the players, who staged comical, bawdy tales in brightly-colored costumes. With time, though, the costumes' colors faded and the players drifted away one by one until there was only Faith and the old man who had brought the players together. He was a sad man, and she watched him die, but she would tell me no more about him than that. Eventually, she found her way to the sea.

After Faith leaves, promising to return soon with more meat and perhaps some stew, I wonder if it is such a bad thing, after all, to die alone.

SPRING REVEALS THE SEA to be a sheet of gold at dawn. I am beginning to forget you, Lushan. I am now writing a letter to Ursula, one I might send, if I can discover words that explain things, or, lacking explanation, offer apology. The image that shadows my eyes now is not of Lushan's face, but of Ursula's back as she carried Blin in her arms to safety outside the house. It is the last image I have of her, because after I escaped Lushan, after flames fell from the roof and covered Lushan — after I dashed outside as he burned — I did not see Ursula anywhere. She had escaped and carried my son with her deep into the center of the city. She did not see me run out of the house, she did not hear my cries to her, she did not know I hid in the shadows and the smoke. I am sure she thinks I stayed behind to watch what had been wrought, and in my dreams I do stay behind — I stand on the edge of the fire, my skin searing, and I stare at Lushan's screaming face as the flames devour him.

I have burned you in my mind, Lushan, and I have watched the son and the woman I loved disappear into safety. That is the story I will cling to, the story I will remember, the story I am not afraid to tell.

* * *

FAITH KNOCKS GENTLY on the door. I open it and she steps in, breathing hard, but smiling. She says she has brought wonders to cook today. We will feast on wonders. I tell her to rest while I unpack what she has brought, but she brushes me away and excitedly opens the sack to show me whale meat and bright, plump sea vegetables. She says that once upon a time the mermaids fought ravenous warriors away from the treasures of the sea, but one day, after the sea turned bright red at sunset with the blood of men and mermaids, the fighting stopped and the mermaids and men ate together in happiness.

A good story, I say.

Faith shrugs. The details of the story were better once, but she has forgotten them.

THE SUN RISES. Faith walks up the long beach toward my hut, a heavy sack carried on her curved, ancient back. We will tell each other stories, and perhaps I will tell her about my husband who burned to death and the woman who saved my son from the fire, and we will smile sadly at the vagaries of chance and life. Perhaps I will burn these mermaid scales before Faith arrives, and all our stories henceforth will remain unwritten, will live and die quickly in the air, will depend entirely on our memories and the ink of our dreaming.

Or perhaps you fled the fire, Lushan, and chased me into the forest, then, defeated by the darkness, you stopped and returned to the city and to Blin and even, perhaps, to Ursula, who still, perhaps, sings a song of Lorelei, who drowned in the spring, because no-one could bother to save her.

JoSelle Vanderhooft
Dissecting Ophelia

People write too many poems about me.
Too many lays
too many manifestos
too many self-help books.
They slice whole forests round about their feet
to graph (they say)
my spleen or, perhaps, to chart
my lights' parabolas which overspread
the stream that ended me
like a purple sail.

Each has his guess,
her theory
and their thoughts.
Each and every night they plot them out
against the cork board:
a red tack for my father,
blue for Laertes,
purples for the royals, and at length
a black pushpin for Hamlet.
I laugh at the cliché
and they look up
as if a bird rushed past.

They make their research plans,
and then they say
"Tomorrow we'll work out

the final bugs."
The latch click-locks,
the lights snap down like dusk.
I am left alone
corpse on a table
lovely, lovely bones
blue and waiting for the knife.

I wait a bit
a little
just to be sure
so there are no close calls —
a missing purse
a wallet by the HCL suspension.
Once, one of them, a male
forgot his keys.
To this day I worry that he saw my sheet
flutter as he entered, but I can't be sure.

I wait until the clock ticks past
an hour
or two.
Depends on how I feel.
Then my eyes spring like clocks.
I creak to life
and cast aside my cover like swan wings.

I'm always naked,
blue as death and glaciers.
My feet leave watermarks upon the tiles
as I read their calculations.
My laughter shakes the white boards.

Do they think that I'm so easy to sound
because I am Ophelia?
I look again. What did they make tonight?
Like real scientists they have set down
each known quantity.
There is a slanting willow.
There is a brook.
There are daisies woven in a rope,
gowns like Venetian glass.
There are snatches of old tunes.
There is an undertoe
(of course, why not).
And last of all, someone thought to include
my very own Queen Gertrude.

It's so sweet
I almost hate to rub it out, and yet
I do it, anyway.

They want to know.
They must know.
They. must. know
My strengths and weaknesses as if I
truss-like stood above the stream
and peered into its depths like Narcissus.

They must know
They must know
Why my backbone did not stand
firm as a martini sword
why my throat was closed
with phlegm, not bile

(brown or black, but black's always in season)
and why, and why
and why why why
why why

I am not He who caught
the conscience of the king upon a spit
and shoved it in the fire.
Why I dared to run
mad as the wind instead
of raising up an army as He did
to batter the usurper's gates
around His ankles.

Oh they have their favorites too, you know.
I was in love
I was already mad
and this — my favorite
made by a high-heeled dame
in Prada and Armani —
that I was a girl
a-tangled in the mobbled queen's embrace
like fishing flies to hooks.

I've read them each and every night
and each and every morning they come in
to find their whiteboard smashed
their markers bent
their pins stuck in the ceiling and their files
waved and dripping still
like mascara.

They sigh and clean
and swear some other time
that it will be different.
One day they'll keep their work.
One day they'll be ready to cut
inside the pretty corpse that even now
smiles underneath her sheets
silent as the river, still
as the wind in unstopped holes.

Ian Watson
Saint Louisa
of the Wild Children:
an Annotated Hagiography

"THOSE KIDS!" DECLARED BARBARA. "Louisa, you have the patience of a saint."

"Hmm!" said her friend. "And at this rate pretty soon I'll be martyred! What I should have on my gravestone is: *She Was Torn Apart by Wild Children.* Like wild horses, but *busier.*"

Louisa's Jay and Ritchie, three and four respectively, were both hyperactive. Toys survived unbroken for only a few days, or hours. The kids were forever running round, bouncing off the walls. Fatal to let Jay or Ritchie out of your sight for too long — the kitchen floor would be covered with sugar one day, rice the next. Such a fuss to feed the boys while they watched video cartoons (without them watching cartoons, an impossibility). Screaming fits at the least frustration. What's more, ear-ache and fevers and stomach-ache: the boys seemed to take turns. Or else one of them would be having nightmares, and might wet the bed. Most nights Louisa lost sleep. She was certainly losing weight. However, she was strong. She ran everywhere. Upstairs, downstairs, to the shops and back again.

Mind you, the boys were her treasures too. She had *created* them – with the assistance of husband Dan —

from out of her own body, so that made them utterly precious to her. And they could also behave very sweetly. So she never smacked them nor shouted at them, but was always loving and gentle. And very imaginative: she played wonderful games with the boys and told them fantastic stories of pirates and fairies and cowboys. Indeed Louisa reproached herself for not devoting *sufficient* attention to her boys. Attention was what they needed and craved. Friends who knew her home situation thought she was crazy. They would promptly have put the boys on Ritalin. At times her husband thought she was crazy. As an alternative to throwing up his hands, Dan would shout at the boys and even spanked their bottoms occasionally.

Louisa was quite realistic and humorous about the way Jay and Ritchie were wearing her down.

"Wild horses," she repeated tragi-comically, for formerly she had shown promise as an actress. But now she was a mum. Or maybe a Supermum, though sometimes she called herself a disaster because of the boys — was she bringing them up wrongly?

"What *is* it with wild horses?" asked Barbara. Barbara had called in after a visit to the hairdresser resulting in red streaks in her chestnut hair as though she had been assaulted by an eagle. "I mean, we say wild horses wouldn't drag me to see *Star Wars IX*, but why should wild horses want to drag anyone anywhere?"

"They could easily drag *me* — I haven't been to the cinema for four years."

A crash and cries from upstairs caused Louisa to vanish promptly, leaving Barbara alone with coffee cup. A few minutes later Louisa returned, carrying a doll whose head had been torn off — she encouraged her boys to play with dolls as well as with more masculine toys. Quickly she binned the ruined doll and swallowed her coffee, now cool.

"While I was upstairs I googled — "

Dan dealt in rare stamps, coins, and medals at his small shop in town but many orders came by e-mail, consequently the computer was always switched on. Louisa handled quite a lot of the correspondence and invoices so she could be up till two in the morning if Dan was too busy checking values in catalogues.

"How *do* you fit it all in?"

"By doing things fast," said Louisa. "Anyway, I googled quickly. In Greek mythology Hippolytus was dragged to death by his own chariot's horses when they bolted. That must be the origin of Saint Hippolytus being dragged or pulled apart by wild horses as a martyrdom — though probably he's fictitious, what with his name being the same as in the Greek myth. And then this became a nasty form of execution, called quartering alive. According to Gregory of Tours in the sixth century Queen Brunehild's limbs were tied to the tails of four horses which were driven apart slowly, and the Thuringians, whoever they were, killed two hundred Frankish women the same way, and Lucas van Leyden did a drawing of a woman being pulled to pieces by horses in about 1530, oh the poor dear woman, and when Damiens was tortured to death in 1757 for trying to kill Louis XV the French used cart-horses, only the horses weren't strong enough until the executioner took a knife to the poor man's sinews, bless his soul — "

"Wow, all that info *plus* a beheaded doll."

"Well, I have a good memory. Anyway, none of these horses were *wild* — unless that's because they were being whipped. Well, I had this image in my mind of captured wild stallions rearing and bucking — but that's nonsense. How would the Thuringians, whoever they were, have eight hundred captive wild horses at hand?"

"I thought you said two hundred."

"One for each limb, silly! Poor women. I can easily imagine mums being pulled apart by wild children, their own."

"You'd need *four* children for that."

"Not if they were Jay and Ritchie — two will do! That should definitely be on my gravestone."

"Don't be morbid — though you *are* looking skinny."

"I'm all right, I'll survive. Promise me those words will be on my grave!"

Louisa often expressed wild fancies, so Barbara duly promised. Louisa even scribbled the words down and signed them, quite in the form of a Will, then she stuck the paper in a drawer and forgot all about it. She had a good memory for some things although she was forgetful of others, such as where her purse or house keys were.

Barbara remembered Louisa's words clearly. For some while now Barbara had belonged to a creative writing group of housewives, which Louisa had no time to join, and an instructor had said, "Ladies, there's inspiration everywhere."

LOUISA DID NOT SURVIVE. Shortly after, a stroke carried her off. Such a gentle-sounding event, a stroke. *Stroke my hair, will you? Oh that's lovely.* Well, a brain haemorrhage is quite a small event. On the other hand, a stroke of lightning is very violent. Different strokes for different folks.

Jay and Ritchie were genuinely very contrite. Dan was furious as well as grief-stricken, and confronted by a daunting task, looking after the boys. Barbara immediately began consoling and helping Dan — non-sexually and with no intention of replacing Louisa — and quickly located the signed piece of paper.

At Louisa's funeral Barbara[1] read out an imaginative eulogy, which she had penned on parchment, beside the open grave, then she threw the parchment on to the coffin to accompany a wreath of roses from Dan[2],

---

[1] A "Barbara" being named as best friend may refer to Hanna-*Barbara* video cartoons (such as Scooby Doo) which assisted Louisa in feeding her children.

[2] "Dan" is a Japanese title for a master of martial arts, i.e. a perfect man, thus a suitable spouse for a saint. A suitable spouse would also be a master of marital arts. But the name may also allude to the Biblical Dan(iel) who was put into a den of lions, whose mouths an angel glued shut so that they did not tear Dan apart — by contrast with Louisa's martyrdom at the hands of wild children. This is a subtle text. Note that one of Louisa's alleged miracles was "the taming of wild horses," though this is probably apocryphal.

while the two boys wept.[3] Of course worms would nibble the parchment, leaving only various fragments.

TWO CENTURIES LATER civilisation collapsed due to global warming, water wars, oil wars, mass starvation (not masturbation[4]), plagues, limited nuclear warfare, and a few other calamities. One day during a tempest a wandering priest dressed in dog-fur stumbled into the graveyard near the ruins of a town. Most of the gravestones had fallen over but one remained upright, offering some shelter from the soaking northerly gale.

---

[3] Many people thought that her boys were lovely, including family friends, grandparents, and a lot of visitors too. Jay and Ritchie could be very endearing. When one time Louisa fell ill (which wasn't possible for longer than a day, even if she had pneumonia), Jay pulled a blanket over his Mum as she lay on the sofa, and brought her some milk. "Are you going to die?" he asked her. "Well, don't!" A week later, Ritchie must have been learning at nursery school about the Blessed Virgin Mary, whom God took up bodily to Heaven, because suddenly he asked Louisa, "Mummy, are you a virgin?" What a question! Were Ritchie's school chums talking about sex already? It took Louisa almost five seconds to deduce the connection.

[4] Please be careful when you read this account aloud to illiterate audiences, because they may easily mishear at this point. They may decide that excessive use of porn sites caused the downfall of civilisation due to too much enthusiasm for virtual sex on the part of home computer users and loss of interest in actual copulation. This would be a "masturbation plague."

Father O'Connor goggled at the inscription on the marble headstone that was saving him from terminal hypothermia, and crossed himself.

> DEARLY BELOVED LOUISA
> TORN APART BY WILD CHILDREN
> SHE WAS A SAINT

When the tempest died away, in gratitude for his salvation Father O'Connor[5] pledged to devote himself to the cult of Saint Louisa, if this already existed — and, if not, he himself would found a cult by gathering evidence of other miracles associated with Louisa.

The post-apocalyptic mid-24th century was a bit like the Middle Ages. Instead of random stuff from classical antiquity, mythified and much misunderstood, there was random stuff from 21st century civilisation.

LET'S CONSIDER the principal attributes and miracles credited to Saint Louisa. To inject a personal note, I'm trained in the tradition of the Bollandists, those scholars of the Society of Jesus who devoted themselves to a *scientific* and systematic analysis of the lives of the saints. Bollandists are named after John Bolland, who was described as "a Balloon," by which I suppose that his girth was considerable, unless this

---

[5] To "con" means "to direct the course of a ship" and "to examine something carefully," both of which are appropriate to O'*Con*nor's intention. However, be aware that a "con" is also a swindle which involves persuading gullible people to believe in something false.

meant he was full of hot air.[6]

Firstly, Louisa is said to have been "a teacher." However, this is true of many saints who preached, and whose lives teach us all a lesson. Maybe she was not a teacher in the strict sense of the word — she would seem to have been too busy with other things!

Secondly, "she danced [with] flamingos." This seems unlikely because most flamingos live in the shallow waters of lakes in Africa, and Saint Louisa isn't identified as being a missionary. However, flamingos *do* perform elaborate courtship dances (and when mating the male tucks his legs up under the female's wings, so that she must bear all his weight).[7]

Thirdly, "she played the guitar and she sang and wrote songs." The best known of these is her cheerful anthem, *You are my sunshine, my only sunshine*, which is sung on Louisa's feast day.[8]

---

[6] *Walloons*, not Balloons, were the inhabitants of part of the land formerly known as Belgium. The headquarters of the Bollandists were in Belgium.

[7] The Spanish word for flamingo is *flamenco*, which is also the name of a colourful and passionate type of dancing. [Flamenco-style dancing has recently been incorporated into Saint Louisa's feast day.] The idea of Saint Louisa (who might have become an actress?) being able to dance flamenco makes more sense than a connection with African birds. However, where saints are concerned, quite often locations and events and persons become confused together. This was true in ancient times, and it became true again due to the collapse of civilisation.

[8] Alternatively, this song was composed by the Governor of the erstwhile "state" of Louisiana, as one of its two

Fourthly, "she fought a worm," i.e. a dragon, from the ancient word *wyrm*. Probably this is a borrowing of the legend of St George rescuing a maiden from a dragon, an event which led to thousands of conversions.[9]

Fifthly, she was a "pregonera." That title probably refers to her being a *mother* of two boys, with whom she had formerly *been pregnant*.

Sixthly, and most importantly, "she was torn apart by wild children." We all know the much-reprinted illustration (in comic-strip format of six frames) showing Saint Louisa in a forest discovering post-apocalyptic feral children running on all fours, then tending to them, taming them, teaching them to walk reasonably upright, etc. The final frame shows Louisa's martyrdom. She's suspended between four teams of (presumably ungrateful) ferocious feral children. Ropes attach to her wrists and ankles. The teams of children are pulling in different directions. Probably this image is copied from the Lucas van Leyden engraving of 1530 and may not originally

official songs. Father O'Connor may have hijacked this song for the Cult because "Louisiana" sounds as though it might mean "land of Louisa" or even "state (of mind) of Louisa," and because that song uplifts the spirits. [*You are my sunshine* isn't the usual type of flamenco song. But it can perhaps be classed as a *solearia*.]

[9] The so-called Barbara Fragment mentions a "computer" as being part of Louisa's everyday life. Due to the scarcity nowadays of rare raw materials and reliable power supplies, we lack such a device, but apparently worms could live and breed inside "computers," which made them work badly.

have been the final frame of the story at all, but may have been substituted. Personally I imagine a final frame in which Saint Louisa, her halo bright, sits amidst happy rescued children to whom she devoted her life.[10] That is the image we should have in our minds. And personally I believe that "torn apart" refers to how powerfully she was affected by the sufferings of unfortunate children. But then, I'm a scientifically-minded revisionist.

IN MY HUMBLE OPINION the "Barbara Fragment," which recently came to light, is ingeniously written so as to conceal information about Saint Louisa within a banal context. This may have been due to persecution and a need for secrecy in the early days of the cult. Adherents would only pay attention to certain key words such as "patience . . . screaming . . . strong," and so forth. They would ignore the rest.[11]

---

[10] In what was formerly Mexico, Louisa is usually known as "Santa Luisa de los niños feroces," emphasizing the ferocity of the children. Another phrase describing the children is "niños salvages." This doesn't mean that Louisa/Luisa "salvaged" the children from the wild. "Salvages" is a Spanish adjective meaning wild in the sense that the children were uncultivated, or else that they were "savage" and "brutal." Mexicans are said to be morbid as well as exuberant, as witnessed by their "Day of the Dead" fiestas, so they may prefer to accentuate the savagery of Louisa/Luisa's fate.

[11] The ultimate source of the Cult may also *be* the Barbara Fragment itself, rather than O'Connor's alleged epiphany at a gravestone. It is even possible,

* * *

IT IS UNSEASONABLY CHILLY, windy, and overcast for springtime in Spain. Wearing blue jeans and a long brown coat and a white scarf, Luisa walks up the steeply sloping narrow street of the village in company with her husband, Paco the pianist, who looks very posh, and their American writer friend whose novel Luisa is translating. The two little boys run ahead.

When they arrive at the crowded square, a blue-uniformed brass band of young people strikes up. Yet another rocket leaps into the sky, fired from a small metal launcher strapped to a man's arm, and thunder rolls around the mountains. Drinkers fill the long terrace of the Miapolo café. Stalls sell toys and jewellery and watches; sausages sizzle, to be served in buns. A stream of newcomers admire the Queens of Honour in their bright bountiful dresses.

Soon Luisa will be reading the speech she has written in honour of the village. An honour for her too, to be chosen as *pregonera*, inaugurating the patron saint's day fiesta with her *pregón*! Soon

---

contrariwise, that the Barbara Fragment is sheer invention. What has survived from the previous civilisation is random and chaotic. Therefore Louisa may never have existed — nevertheless that piece of invention has become actuality in the minds of many believers, as is true of numerous fictional personalities surviving from the preceding epoch, such as James Double-Oh Seven, Hercules Poirot, and Iñigo Montoya, to name but a few. Accounts of their adventures are believed to be true.

flower-decorated effigies will be wheeled around the streets.

"A little bit like your very own feast day, eh!" the American writer enthuses.

"Oh no, it is the village that matters," says Luisa, who is often amazed if people pay much attention to her. "I am no one. I am just a footnote."

"A footnote," he muses. "Hmm . . . "

Constance Cooper
Cities of Salt and Ice

Upon the sere Saharan plain a thousand years ago,
Beneath its cloudless blue unblinking vault
The city of Taghaza grew, where nothing else would
    grow
With all its buildings fashioned out of salt.

No place of sparkling spires, this, nor palaces of
    white,
No crystal terraces, or columns grand —
But humble huts that huddled on a desiccated site,
With walls gray-pitted by the desert sand.

True, salt was treasure then. Along the dusty road
    that ran
From this grim town to thriving Timbuktu
The gritty blocks were carried out by camel caravan
And brought in trade a kingly revenue.

As for the populace within this town of salten brick,
Slave laborers, in desolation penned —
They spent their days in quarries weighted down
    with spade and pick,
Their nights, enwalled by wealth they could not
    spend.

So we, now exiled from that world to mine this
    frozen rock,
Crouch, cold in spirit, in our caves of ice
While cargo ships come down to take away each
    bitter block
To stations where it brings a sterling price.

I think of the Taghazan slaves, celled in that barren
    waste
And feel our kinship keen across the years
Salt or ice, it matters not in what we are encased
Our prisons are united in our tears.

Gary Every
Sakhmet the Destroyer

The sun hangs high in the sky,
more powerful than anything else in the heavens.
In ancient mythology
the beast which represents the sun
is the golden haired goddess lioness.
When the lion roars all the animals scatter
like the stars disappearing from the light of the sun.

The sun has no shadow,
it creates only light;
it is the presence of others
which gives the universe shade.
When the sun sets on the horizon;
ending the day,
it takes the light with it
and it is we who are left in the dark.

The moon waxes, wanes, dies
and is reborn.
The moon knows both light and shadow,
the push and pull of the tides,
the menstrual cycle.
The beast representing the moon
in bronze age mythology
is the serpent,
a creature who sheds his skin;
understanding death and rebirth,

living the duality,
moving fluidly through time,
swimming effortlessly across the universe.
These are the thoughts that I was thinking
while walking through the museum,
traversing an exhibit of Egyptology.

My stepdaughter stares,
peering past freckles and eyeglasses
at the giant statue of a lioness with a human body.
According to Egyptian legend,
Sakhmet the Destroyer was vengeful.
She was tricked while drunk
on sweet red pomegranate wine
and she became angry; very very angry.
She needed to be consoled
in order to be convinced
to spare life,
all life,
so the world could continue turning.

My stepdaughter tugs on my hand
and I lower my head.
She whispers in my ear
"Usually those kinds of statues
are always boys."
She stares in awe.
Later, we buy an overpriced gift shop statue
a miniature replica of Sakhmet the Destroyer.

During the drive home
the sun sets on the horizon,
the clouds filled with glorious colors.
We will not drive in darkness tonight
for tonight the moon shines bright,
lighting the way.
Samantha sits inside her seat belt,
cuddling her Sakhmet statue.
Someday soon, she will grow into a woman
and when she does I want her to be a lioness.
Because, someday I will dissolve into nothing
like a raindrop falling in the ocean
and when I do
I want sweet little Samantha
to be able to destroy the entire universe
and every one in it,
including you —
if she has to.

Charles Saplak
Cemetery Seven

T HE MOUNTAIN TOWN where I grew up, back in the
West Virginia of the early 30's, was served by six
graveyards — or so I thought. While still a youth, I
learned what few in our town knew, what fewer still
ever discussed out loud. I learned that we were
served by a seventh graveyard, a secret graveyard. I
was destined to make three trips there.

CRAWLEY WAS LIKE HUNDREDS of other small towns,
dominated by mining and logging. In the center of
town was a wood-framed train station which served
the Chesapeake and Ohio and Norfolk Southern lines.
Near it were the courthouse and jail, into which
Sheriff Chet Wilson would throw drunken miners and
woodhicks every Saturday night.

Crawley had a business district: Merchants and
Miners Savings Bank, the Ittman Company Store, the
only place where Ittman employees — and that was
just about everybody — could trade scrip for ridicu-
lously overpriced goods, and the blacksmith and
wainwright shops. Occupying a full block near the
center of town was the Ittman mansion and grounds.
Outside the center of town were churches and fore-
men's houses; beyond those shantytowns where
Coloreds, Italians, Poles, Hungarians, and others
lived in tight little clusters.

Around the outskirts were scattered the six

graveyards: Gethsemane (Baptist), Gethsemane (Methodist), Eternal Remembrance (the Colored graveyard), Gethsemane Memory Garden (Nazarene), the potter's field, and the Catholic graveyard. (A Roman Catholic Church, Sacred Heart of Mary, stood outside town. Technically, Crawley was a mission just like the China or the Congo, and so rated a missionary from the Archdiocese of Wheeling.)

The seventh graveyard lay out in the surrounding hills, the low, blunt, timeworn Appalachian hills, ancient beyond history. They predate law, science, and religion. It's important that you know these facts, that you get an idea of the inner and outer landscape of the town of Crawley, a place nestled in dark forested hills where sunlight struggles to penetrate, a town of Germans who still told Grimm Tales, freed slaves who still told Da Goblin Woman stories, Czechs who still crossed themselves at the sounds of wolves, Hungarians who amputated the legs and decapitated the corpses of suicides, Irish who by day told jokey tales of leprechauns and by night told darker tomes of Picts, Mannikins, and Danish torture, both given and received . . . .

If you can remember these facts then my experiences with the Seventh graveyard will be much more sensible, much more story-like, and therefore much easier to forget . . . .

MY FATHER, JAMES HARPER, SENIOR, was the only doctor in the town of Crawley. By the time I was thirteen I had often been impressed into service to help hold down some drunken miner sliced open in a brawl at the town whorehouse, or to assist in sawing crushed limbs from unlucky railroad men or wood-hicks. I also had to occasionally visit my schoolmates while they lay up with chickenpox or appendicitis, earning a measure of respect a one hundred and twenty pound, five-foot-five boy normally wouldn't get. I'd even assisted my father when he tried and failed to save my mother from influenza.

I believed I had seen it all and had developed an iron constitution, strong stomach, and a stony mask through which I could look on the pain of others in a detached manner. That changed one night of my thirteenth summer.

Even in the isolation of Crawley we had our share of epidemics: flu, diphtheria, rubella, and worse. While these cut the population they also brought into the world occasional "defected" children. It was an unspoken understanding that many of these children were left to die of neglect. It was also possible that many were killed shortly after birth by their families, their midwives, or by the attending physician.

But some survived.

Perrine Couer was a deaf mute girl, and as an infant had been left before the altar at Sacred Heart. She was adopted by the nuns there. It probably would have been possible for them to place her in a nearby home. Children were a valuable commodity with homes to be maintained and fields to be worked. Perhaps they sensed that any volunteers to adopt the deaf girl had this in mind, to use her for coarsest labor. For whatever reason, the sisters kept her and attempted to teach her to read, to write, and to understand their catechism.

Perrine grew into a plain but unusual looking girl. I remember her as enormously animated, somewhat wild-looking. She seemed to glow with an inner life. She had a great curiosity about the world around her, but she strained against the cage of silence in which she lived.

Once I was returning home from one of my expeditions into the forest, either trout fishing or rabbit hunting. As I walked past Sacred Heart of Mary Church I whistled. (Was I happy, or was it an unconscious reflex caused by being within sight of the granite angels and marble Virgin Marys sitting on the green grass of the churchyard?)

A bobwhite answered me, and I replied to him. We called back and forth for a few moments, then the maniac song of a mockingbird drowned us out. I looked up and there she stood — Perrine stared at me in profound puzzlement. I realized sheepishly that I must have been making supremely weird facial expressions.

When I realized that she didn't know what I was doing, I hooked my thumbs together and made a wings-flapping gesture, then spread my hands to indicate the birds in the trees.

Profound sadness and wonder flashed across her face; it occurred to me then that she may not have previously been aware that birds sing. Her face was animated by such longing, my heart very nearly broke then and there. Then her eyes lit up as she looked at me with what I could only interpret as admiration, and joy at what I was able to do.

After that day I dreamed about her often — such is the life of a thirteen year old boy.

ONE DUSTY AND HUMID summer night my father and I were called to the Sacred Heart of Mary Rectory. I gawked at the portrait of Pope Pius XI, the plaster statue of the Virgin Mary, the iron Jesus nailed to an oak crucifix and hung on a wall where sunsets streamed onto it through scarlet stained glass.

The rectory bedroom was simple and plain, and of course over the head of its bed was another crucifix nailed to the wall. Lying on the bed wrapped in a clean sheet was Perrine. She was unconscious; her lips were drawn back, and black blood decorated her gums. The left side of her face was swelling and darkening.

She wore a simple cotton dress. Scowling, my father lifted it by the hem. He nodded at the blood between her legs (she wore no undergarments) as if he expected to see just that.

"Stay here, James, and call for me if she wakes up or stirs."

Father left the room for a moment to talk to the priest, Father MacGuire. I could hear their voices but I didn't pay attention. I couldn't take my eyes from her bruised face. I was repulsed but fascinated. Without thinking I took her hand — so small! — in mine. There was blood under her tiny fingernails. I rubbed her wrist and whispered.

Her head turned slightly and her eyelids fluttered as she regained consciousness. She looked at me as the mists fell away.

And she shrieked, a grunting rasping shriek of a deaf mute.

My father, Father MacGuire, and one of the nuns came into the room. Perrine jerked her hand from mine and tried to sit up on the bed. My father turned to her and said to me over his shoulder, "You'd better leave, James. This poor child's terrified of a sight of a young man."

I left. I got outside to the cool night air. Then I started to shake uncontrollably, as hot tears streamed down my cheeks.

THE ITTMAN HOUSE was the largest and nicest in Crawley. They had their pick of the servants, ignorant wives and daughters of miners who would work eighteen hours for a quarter dollar. Spruce from their sawmill built their walls; coal from their mines heated their rooms. When a man drove a nail or a woman sewed a shirt for the Ittman family they did so with the understanding that a word from Mr. Ittman could ensure that they'd either have work in Crawley for the rest of their lives, or else never work there again.

I don't pretend to preach about what such wealth and power can do to a person; nor can I state any facts about Josephus Ittman, the patriarch, nor his seventeen-year-old son, Duane, nor any of the Ittman family. Likewise, I wasn't there when Sheriff Wilson and Father MacGuire confronted the elder Mr. Ittman, but I did listen in when the two visited my father that evening.

Our home was a two-story, with grills set in the

floors of the upper rooms to allow hot air from the furnace to circulate. One grill in my room was in the corner over the dining area. When Sheriff Wilson and Father MacGuire came in I was dismissed to my room. Once there I crept straight to the grill and eased my weight down as slowly and as carefully as possible. It was too hot for father to brew coffee, so he poured three glasses of Scotch whiskey for himself and his two guests. I knew Chet Wilson wouldn't hesitate, but I was slightly surprised to see the priest accept, and I noticed that he did with shaking hands. I pressed my face to the floor, and caught fragments of the conversation.

" . . . didn't deny it, by God. That boy's a bad seed . . . ."

" . . . threatened you, threatened me . . . Ittman thinks he owns the world . . . ."

" . . . disrespectful little bastard . . . smirked at me . . . scratches on his face . . . ."

" . . . buys and sells the Church, buys and sells the sheriff . . . ."

" . . . our only chance . . . ."

" . . . joked about burning in Hell . . . ."

" . . . appeal to the pagan thing . . . ."

" . . . offered to give us a nigger to lynch, if that would make us feel better . . . ."

" . . . he laughed about burning in Hell . . . ."

" . . . said he'd have my job, said he'd ride you out of town . . . ."

" . . . scratches on his face . . . ."

And then my father looked up toward the grill. I don't know if I'd made a sound upon making the connection between the scratches on Duane Ittman's face and the blood under Perrine Coeur's nails, or if my father had just reached out with his intuition and sensed that I was there.

I crept away from the grill and slid into my bed. With the jumbled perspective of a thirteen-year-old I wondered if I really knew a boy who had raped and beaten a deaf-mute girl — and I wondered if I would be in trouble for eavesdropping.

Eventually I heard the Sheriff and Priest leave, heard them sent off with quiet goodbyes, heard my father's steady footsteps on the stairs.

He knocked softly, then opened the door slightly.

"I'm getting you up early tomorrow, James, so get some rest. And when I get you up I want you to get some gear ready for camping."

Of course I barely slept.

It was a muggy summer morning, with pollen drifting and coating the picket fences and board sidewalks of the town, and with the thick air promising a hot, hot day. At dawn we set out for — for what? The only explanation my father gave me was, "This is about that girl."

I brought out my bamboo rod and my wicker creel.

"Leave those," Father said.

I didn't understand. "Then do I need to pack some more food? How many days do we need for? What do you want me to take for us to eat?"

"Listen up, James. Forget the food, forget the fishing, and forget about asking questions. You wouldn't even be going out with us but you're not a child. You've seen too much and you've been through too much. While we're on this business you just shut up and keep your eyes and ears open."

I looked into his face and saw something I'd *never* seen there before.

Fear.

JUST OUTSIDE TOWN we met Sheriff Wilson and Father MacGuire. Something immediately struck me as odd about Wilson, but I didn't realize what it was at first. After looking him over for a few seconds I realized that he wasn't wearing the double-action Colt revolver he usually carried in a hip holster.

The oddness about Father MacGuire I noticed right away. Instead of his Roman Collar and black garb he wore denim work pants and shirt, along with well-broken-in leather boots.

The two men just nodded at my father and me, then we turned toward the forest. Before the sun was even halfway to its zenith we were out of town and off the roads and trails, with Sheriff Wilson in the lead, pushing through the tangle of forest.

We probably covered twenty miles that first day. We didn't speak; we didn't eat when we stopped to rest; that night we didn't have a fire. I was tired, cold at night, hot during the day, and hungry all the time, but I didn't complain. Although they didn't explain it to me, I sensed that we were on a mission of justice.

JOKES ASIDE, WITHIN A FOREST one never really notices individual trees. I knew enough to recognize mockernut, hackberry, Virginia pine, mountain and striped maples, and others. I would never have imagined that any certain tree could stand out as worthy of notice.

It was the evening of the second day when we broke into a clearing. Instead of the profuse explosion of old growth which had marked the forest so far, the trees stood in what seemed to be an artificial array, spaced about thirty feet apart.

Central in this odd orchard was a twisted oak, over a hundred feet tall, draped with vines and creepers, but leafless, even then in the middle of summer. We were all quiet as we walked up to stand beneath it. There in the clearing we heard no chittering of squirrels nor singing of birds, nor whine of summer insects. The slightest breeze whispered through the branches; the ground crunched beneath our feet.

I had never been the type, when looking with other kids at clouds, to see any dragons or knights on horseback. I always saw clouds. But that day in that clearing I looked at that oak and saw, in its shape, in the way its branches twisted as if beckoning, in the texture of the bark which seemed like a hundred years' worth of words in an unknown language, something frightening. Something icy needled my spine, and the sweat running down my back felt clammy.

"It's near," Sheriff Wilson said.

My father nodded.

I looked at Father MacGuire. His eyes were wide and his chest was heaving.

The sun, blood red, touched the treetops on the horizon.

"If anybody's going to back out, they'd better say so now," the Sheriff said.

My father shook his head; Father MacGuire croaked, "No."

"You speaking for James?" the Sheriff asked my father.

He nodded. "He's in."

"It's cold," Father MacGuire said.

"Let me see your hand, James," Sheriff Wilson said.

I held out my right hand (the same with which I'd held Perrine's hand). Sheriff Wilson clamped an iron grip around my middle, ring, and small fingers. Father MacGuire took hold of my thumb and index fingers, while my father grabbed my wrist.

I didn't cry out. I didn't know what was coming, but by that stage of the proceedings I was prepared for anything. Father MacGuire took a tin cup from his pack and held it beneath my hand; Sheriff Wilson pulled a folding Barlow and opened it with the fingers of his free hand. As he drew the blade across my palm father squeezed my wrist as if he wanted to crush it.

As the Sheriff took the knife away my father loosened his grip on my wrist and blood, looking black in the twilight, pumped into the cup with a pattering sound.

"That's enough," Wilson said, and the priest drew back the cup. I looked down and realized that the crunching, shifting ground we were standing on beneath the twisted oak was a collection of shattered skulls and broken bones, adorned with mushrooms and decades worth of fallen leaves.

Father MacGuire took a stoppered cruet from his pack. At first I thought it was more blood, but he looked at me and said, "Wine. Don't worry, it hasn't been sanctified."

He added it to the cup of my blood.

SUNSET IN THE MOUNTAINS is a gradual process. The sun disappears but the sky is lit for a time after. The border between darkness and light is uncertain. Father MacGuire, seemingly at the Sheriff's prompting, looked at the three of us, and said a strange thing.

He said, "Faith. Faith is required, but we can't impose our faith upon the world that exists. We have to look squarely at each thing in the world, no matter how seemingly — *unnatural* — that thing should be. And then faith has to be built on our experience. And may God the Father, his Incarnate Son, and the Holy Spirit have mercy on my soul."

When he finished, he raised the cup to his lips, then passed it to my Father.

My father, sounding as if he'd been rehearsing this for days, said, "The physician tends the flesh and stands in awe of the spirit."

That said, he drank, then passed the cup to the Sheriff.

"The Goddess of Justice, bless her, is blind . . . and also lame and deaf and usually crazy," he said, then drank, then smacked his lips. He passed the cup to me, and gave me these instructions: "Tell us everything you know about that girl, then take a drink. Not a big drink; just touch it with the tip of your tongue, really."

And so I did. I closed my eyes, and told the whole thing, starting with the birdcalls, and ending with her mute scream in the bedroom of the rectory.

I tasted the bitter mixture, and held it out to see who would take it.

None of the three men with me did. We all turned as we heard a rustling, creaking, scratching sound from the direction of the trunk of the oak tree. The light was dim but not entirely gone. A gibbous moon was coming out as the sky darkened.

The creature could have been standing there, pressed against the tree, all along. It was roughly human-shaped, tall as the average adult man. It wore no clothes, but its skin was textured like rough bark, and colored like slate. Its face was structured as if it didn't have to conform to any internal skull. The eyes appeared to be patches of fungus.

"The story did it," the Sheriff said. My father put his hands on my shoulders. Father MacGuire started speaking Latin in a low, rhythmic voice.

The creature took the tin cup from my hand (its skin, harsh and scratchy, brushed mine). It drained it in one gulp, then dropped the cup. It wandered back toward the oak, and whether it took a position there or went to some other place in the darkness, I couldn't tell.

"It's going to help us," the Sheriff said.

I WAS PREPARED to spend a restless night. We settled down there in the middle of the orchard (although we made sure to get clear of the oak tree and its ringing carpet of skulls) to a cold camp. Off in the darkness the creature walked, occasionally digging or gathering things. I remember thinking that I could never get to sleep as the priest murmured his prayers, Wilson tossed and turned, and my father sat occupying his hands by weaving tiny strands from vines into miniature cages. And that's the last that I remember of that night, as I put my head down and fell asleep.

THE SUN WAS UP when my father shook me awake. "Come on," he said. "We're obligated to watch this."

I blinked back at the light. *Obligated*, he said. As I got up I rubbed my eyes and noticed that he had bandaged my hand as I had slept.

I walked with father to where Sheriff Wilson and Father MacGuire stood beneath the twisted oak. The creature squatted cross-legged beside the trunk, seemingly oblivious to our presence. I got a closer look at it in the light.

While I watched it absently pulled a strip of bark from its "face." It seemed to be concentrating, tilting its head to listen to some inner music.

Off in the distance I heard a commotion in the forest. The air in that creature's orchard was so still that we could hear the sound coming closer, closer, closer.

After about a minute of listening to the approaching sound, we saw a human figure break into the clearing.

At least it looked human. It was torn and scratched and bloody, as if it had been dragged through the forest. It had once worn clothes, but they were now little more than shreds. Its arms and legs jerked puppet-like as if it weren't in control. Its face was a slack mask of pain and confusion.

It was Duane Ittman.

Father MacGuire made a gesture as if to reach out to Ittman, but Sheriff Wilson held him back. Duane staggered up to the twisted oak and tugged on one of the creepers. He looped it around his neck several times. I glimpsed his eyes at one point. His look was hideous. His look told me that he regarded his own hands as alien agents.

He had the vine looped several times around his own neck and was standing tiptoe, when something unexpected happened (if the events so far had been expected by Wilson, MacGuire, and my own father).

The creature, which had been squatting and watching with apparent disinterest suddenly sprang to its feet and strode forward to put its hands around Ittman.

"What's he doing?" my father asked.

"Dear God, he's taking him down!" Father Mac-Guire said. "We've accused an innocent man!"

"No!" Sheriff Wilson said. "He has something else in mind!"

The creature dragged Ittman to a spot spaced away from its other trees. We four followed. As we watched the creature held the vines which were still wrapped around Ittman's neck in one hand, and frantically scratched at the soil with another. The mole, the ant, and the earthworm had nothing on this creature. It seemed like only a few minutes before he had hollowed out a deep narrow hole and had dragged

Ittman into it. The last I saw of Duane Ittman's face was the screaming mouth, the eyes stretched wide, as the creature scooped dirt over his head.

The creature patted the dirt down, then sat there, as if proud of itself, or as if it had satisfied some urge. The dirt writhed a little, for a few minutes.

At one point I looked away (I tasted the dirt in my mouth, felt the soil over my eyes, felt my own lungs burning for air). My father put a gentle — but firm — hand on the back of my head and forced me to watch the dirt writhe. *Obligated*, he'd said.

As the sun reached its zenith, the dirt had stopped moving, and the creature, without gesture or word or sign, walked away from us and disappeared into the woods.

"Come on," Sheriff Wilson said. "It's finished."

We returned to town.

My father and I never spoke about what we had seen. Sheriff Wilson and Father MacGuire never mentioned it to me either, but on the occasions when I saw them thereafter they treated me differently, without the kindness and smiles adults reserve for children, but with the knowledgeable, sad faces adults offer each other.

Father MacGuire, for his part, grew dour and quiet, as if struggling with some internal question. Within the year he would request and receive assignment to the Belgian Congo. I later heard from a Catholic acquaintance that he'd died there under uncertain circumstances, possibly murdered.

Sheriff Wilson was killed by machine gun fire in

a mine war in 1934, unlucky middleman between strikers and Baldwin-Felts "detectives." One year later, the mine guard system was outlawed in West Virginia, and mine wars became less deadly.

The elder Mr. Ittman never pressed anyone about the disappearance of his son. The whole episode passed into town legend, and people theorized that he'd met an accidental death while fishing or hunting in the hills.

About once a year, in my youth, I had nightmares of being buried alive. (In my old age they decreased to one every few years).

The girl, Perrine, became a recluse. She stayed inside the convent and the church, and to my knowledge, never ventured out again. The kids in town turned her into a whispered legend, the "mad girl" or the "deformed girl" who the Catholics were keeping locked up.

I often found myself straying to that part of town, walking past the church, cooing at the mourning doves or attempting to whistle up a mockingbird. I once thought that I saw a face looking at me from behind a curtained window, but I couldn't be sure.

In the winter of the third year after that fateful summer, she died.

IT WAS TYPICAL FOR US in that valley to not bury the dead which had died in the middle of winter, as the ground often froze solid. I don't know what arrangement my father made, but the morning after Perrine died he woke me up and directed me to once again prepare gear for a trek into the woods.

Perrine was tightly wrapped in a white silk bundle. My father rigged a harness by which we could either divide her weight between us, or could take turns bearing her. A relentless, gentle snow fell on us the whole way. I don't think we spoke a single word to each other.

The creature seemed to have been expecting us.

It had a place all ready. It was a spot spaced from its other trees; a spot which would be sun drenched in summer; a spot which would be sheltered from the wind which could cause a tree to grow crooked.

The creature knelt by the hole while my father and I lowered the silk-shrouded burden into the ground.

"Shouldn't we say something?" I asked.

"Do you know any words? I've been neglectful on what to teach you, I suppose. Probably thought that if you could patch a wound and sew up a cut you'd be prepared for life. Maybe I should have spent more time teaching the right words."

The creature tugged at my father's sleeve. Its skin perfectly matched the overcast and colorless winter day. The effect was to make it appear like nothing so much as an extension of the forest itself.

It pulled my father over toward a stunted, leafless tree about ten feet tall. It bade us to sit beneath its scrawny branches.

The snowflakes continued to drift silently down around us.

The creature snapped branches off the tree and stacked them in a little teepee shape. I didn't see what means it used to start a fire, but it soon had the stack of wood burning.

My father and I appreciated the warmth. The fire popped and squealed and sparked as the creature fed it with wood from the tree. It broke off all the branches then set to work pulling the trunk apart. It didn't stop until the fire roared, and sparks drifted up into the gray, snowy sky. The heat felt good, and warmed my cheeks and nose and outstretched hands. My father's expression was somber, and I soon realized why.

The tree had grown from the same spot in which the creature had, three years earlier, buried Duane Ittman.

Just before my father and I left to return for town, the creature tossed a branch which missed the fire where the rest of the wood lay sizzling and hissing. I picked it up to toss it into the flame.

I felt — or imagined that I felt — the very fiber of the wood squirming in pain, or terror.

THE INTERVENING YEARS were eventful and transforming, not simply for me and for the town of Crawley, but for the world as well. In 1944 I received my M.D. from West Virginia University in Morgantown, just in time to enter the Army as a reserve officer and to eventually participate in the liberation of Buchenwald. The theories of justice, science, medicine, and law with which I'd been educated could not be reconciled with what I saw there, nor with what I was to see five years later at the Chosin Reservoir in Korea.

I had a practice in Huntington, West Virginia for many years, and worked as a lecturer at the Marshall

University Medical College. In 1963 my father passed away from cancer.

I never married.

In the early seventies I traveled back to Crawley, which had become a ghost town. There was no sign of the blacksmith or wainwright shops; some streets had been paved in the intervening years and later became broken; the yards and the streets which had never been paved had been reclaimed by thick weeds. All the company homes were burnt-out, broken-windowed husks. The railroad tracks were overgrown, testifying that N+S and C+O had abandoned that spur. The Ittman mansion was now a shattered castle of snakes and birds.

In my sixties I was still a reasonably fit man, used to hiking and backpacking, and I had come prepared. I locked my car and left it parked behind a small general store near Rupert (the nearest surviving town). As best as my memory and topographic maps could lead me I followed our original path into the thick forest around Crawley.

I saw absolutely no sign of that creature I've since come to think of as the *Arboreteur*, and no sign of his original orchard. Civilization seemed to have won out after all. There were no places in the forest where I could be free of the sounds of airplanes crawling through the sky overhead, or the whisper of automobiles on distant roads. Within the thickest groves of briars I found cracked axe heads, rusted fish hooks, and empty Pepsi cans.

By the evening of the third day I had convinced myself the *Arboreteur* was a confused legend, something I'd imagined; an idle story which had coalesced into something more solid with the passing of the years. I let my campfire burn down and resolved to head back the next morning and to never think of it again.

As I slept Perrine came to me. She slipped her hand back into mine and said — without words of course — *Thank you and goodbye. I'm happy here. Let me go.*

The vision faded as I awoke. There was commotion in the branches of the cedar above me — a proper cedar, I realized, like the African, Lebanese, and Turkish cedars, and not a juniper native to America. A rare tree, rare and out of place.

Within its branches, raucous blue jays, cooing mourning doves, and riotous mockingbirds filled the air with sweet song.

Catherynne M. Valente
The Eight Legs of Grandmother Spider

1

I will go,
said a double-jointed voice
out of the dark.

I will fetch the sun
from the country of fire
and bring it back
safe as bread.

In the black,
the only sound
was icicles jangling
on frozen fur.

No,
said the animals,
huddled one against the other,
Possum will go.
He is bigger than you,
and he can hide the sun in his bristle-tail.

Balanced on her basket-web
over the lightless water,
Spider shrugged
and sighed.

2

      I was four—

four, and you were seventy-two,
in your silver wheelchair
black and green afghan
over corduroyed knees
with my skinny arms
wrapped around you,
and your hands on my new dress.
I curled into sleep on your knitted lap
breathing your smell
of cinnamon and antiseptic cream.

The TV gurgled lazily,
cartoons and mint toothpaste ads
and my hair was tangled
in the pretty beads around your neck
those tight black curls
and my brown ringlets
twisting to make a second chain.

Both of us snored a little,
soft as cats,
covered in light
like your heavy orange rhododendrons,
light drifting in
through the windows
that would have been washed
when you got around to it.

3

In the black,
the only sound
was Possum
whimpering and licking
his pink tail, scalded bald.

I will go,
said a silk-sticky voice
out of the dark.

I will fetch the sun
from the other side of the world
and bring it back
safe as swaddling.

Chattering jaws
gnawed frostbitten bones
and pupils were open pools
in shivering skulls.

No,
said the animals,
groping for purchase
in the shadows.
Buzzard is cleverer than you,
and besides,
he can fly.
He will balance the sun on his head,
like a woman carrying water.

Busy wrapping a bee
in gauze,
Spider shrugged
and sighed.

4

You hands were folded over my shoulders,
the hands of a chicken farmer
who wrung the necks of roosters
up north of Talequah for forty years —
        whose mother
was pale enough to pass,
but for that sleek braided hair
and those too-black eyes,
        whose handsome husband
left her with six children,
        whose red-headed daughters
ran off to Los Angeles together
and came home every night smelling
of movie popcorn and orange soda,
        whose grand-daughter
was a beautiful actress
and went to a grand university,
        whose great-granddaughter
was four,
was four,
and still moved her lips when she read.

5

In the black,
the only sound
was Buzzard
cawing and rubbing
his pink head, scalded
to a bald wrinkle.

I will go,
came a thick-bellied voice
out of the dark.

I will fetch the sun
from the land of light
and bring it back
safe as sealing wax.

Horns butted against antlers
against feathers against fins,
so lost were all things
in the murk of the world.

Go, then,
said the animals
since Possum and Buzzard
were burned up like birch bark.
Go, fetch the sun for us,
we are so cold,
and so blind —
the kittens' eyes do not open,
the larvae do not hatch
the chicks do not break their eggs.

Spry on eight grey legs,
Spider shrugged,
and climbed over the shale,
silk drifting behind her.

6

Later my aunts would tell me
that when I was born
You held me first of anyone
and wept over my dark little head.
They said we looked like a photograph
they have of you,
black-haired infant
in the arms of your mother
in the days when she would whisper
when she knew no one would hear:
aquetsi ageyutsa,
aquetsi uwoduhi ageyutsa.

They said my pupils were open pools;
I up looked at you
and your tears splashed
on my cheeks,
that first evening
in the hospital over the sea
when the white sailboats
were tipped in gold
and rocked like a lullaby on the slow water.

You sang to me
in the white walled maternity ward

whispering and crooning —
but it is a only story I have been told
I can't recall your voice,
or what song it might have been.

7

The sun scorched the basket,
of course.

And her legs, not so different
in thickness
from the coffer-straw,
singed at the tips
like used matches.

But for them,
she put the fire
like a bright ball of dough
into the clay,
and it made of the clay a kiln, '
and it made of the kiln an oven,
and it made of the oven a womb.

For them,
she melted the ice
from her own small, grey body
and with the sun
like a corn-cake frying beneath her,
she boiled herself
into day,
a little dark speck
dwindling
against the sudden blaze.

8

It was so simple and quiet:
                I woke up
and you didn't.

I was four;
I couldn't understand, quite,
but I started to scream,
babbling for you,
tugging at your hands,
your chicken-throttling hands,
your seed-scattering hands,

your sun-stealing hands.

And all I have of you now
is your nose and high forehead
and this sleek hair,
these too-black eyes —
and how I held you last of anyone,
                that you died in my arms
when I was four years old
and the late afternoon sun
lay in your lap like a baby.

Erzebet YellowBoy
Misha and the Months

"THIS MUST STOP," the woman said under her breath as she rose up from her wide bed.

Pots rattled and banged in the dusty kitchen, an ongoing symphony of discord, a concert of metal on metal. It was Marta, of course, doing the chores. Misha counted — one, two, three — she knew that the music would cause Mama to rise up from her afternoon's nap in a fury. The sound of Mama's feet hitting the stairs was drowned by the noise, but Misha felt the vibration of a pending storm and ducked back down into her threads.

"Marta!" Mama's voice was shrill and sharp, as usual. Was her throat incapable of producing a different sound?

"What?" came the tart reply.

Marta was much like a tart, Misha mused between careful stitches. Good to look at on the outside, but with a sting that leaked out when its crust was broken. Someone had left Marta in the oven for too long. Her crust was burnt and cracked all over.

"Must you make such a racket? You should study the art of silence at Misha's feet. And if you don't mind those pots I'll have you sitting at your sister's feet polishing her boots!"

"That girl is not my sister!" Marta slammed iron onto the stove.

"Your father made her your sister when he married me, young woman, and don't you forget who's in charge here."

Misha, from the safe distance of the parlor, could imagine the snarl that surely rested on Mama's thin face. She hated this, hated the unleashing of anger and the cloud of dank air left behind that circled her head like bats, pulling at loose strands of hair with a pinch. She hated, too, that Marta thought so poorly of her. She had tried, more than once, to be her friend, but Marta thought Misha was boring, always at the embroidery, never making a fuss.

"You're not in charge of me!" Marta shouted.

Misha heard the door that led out to the barren herb garden slam, leaving in its wake another rattling of a different sort. She expected that one of these days the door would fall completely from the hinges.

Mama swept into the parlor like the blizzard that had come late yesterday, turning the sky to slate and coloring it with streaks of chalky snow. The little house had been all but buried by morning. Winter was always the worst, now that Papa was gone and with him, all of his stories. Though he was not Misha's true father, he had been kind to her.

Mama sat on the frayed cushion of the settee, gazing at the sparkling trees that stood at frozen attention beyond the window.

"I don't know what we're going to do with that girl," she said to the air.

Misha threaded her needle with red yarn and pulled it through the cotton in a small attempt to relieve the interminable boredom that sucked out the marrow of her aching bones. She wished that she could wash a pot, or go for a walk, or do anything other than this infernal embroidery, but Mama would not hear of it.

"What are you sewing?" Mama asked.

The hoop was held out for inspection, revealing a half-formed landscape dotted with the outline of many birds. Misha hoped the design would make an intricate enough project to carry her through the winter. It had not always been so tedious; when Papa was alive the cold months were made warm and friendly by a big fire in the hearth and tales of his travels for Marta and herself every night. Mama had servants then to do the chores and had plied her own threads with care and skill.

"Pity you aren't beautiful, we could marry you off without a dowry. One less mouth to feed." Misha flinched. Mama didn't realize the pain she caused, for in her mind such thinking was practical and nothing more. Still. It was not Misha's fault that she didn't have Marta's beauty, even darkened, as it was, by the foulest of tempers. Misha put her head back down into her threads and wished they'd both just disappear.

The kitchen door slammed again, open and shut, and the pots rumbled in protest.

"I have got to do something about her." Mama was torn. If Marta went, she and Misha would be doing those chores, but the peace they would gain might make it worth the drudgery.

Misha watched from slitted eyes, her nerves picking up some new cruelty pickling her mother's heart.

"I know just the thing." Mama swooped like a vulture back toward the kitchen.

Marta bent over the blackened hearth, feeding wood from the pile into the already blazing fire. The flames turned her braided hair to molten copper and shone on cheeks gone rosy from the cold. Pity, thought Mama. We could marry this one off in no time if she would just keep her mouth shut.

"Marta," she smiled. "I know how it chafes you to be trapped in the house all winter. I have an errand for you to run."

Marta looked at the woman who called herself her mother. Bone-thin and ugly, she found her, a common wench bloated with false superiority. She hated her. She hated that drab bit of a thing she was supposed to call sister, as well. She flung a pot towards the sink.

Mama winced. "Violets. I want fresh violets on the table tonight."

The wood in Marta's hand clattered to the floor. "Violets?" she spat.

"Do as you're told," Mama replied, her voice cracking like the limbs of a frozen oak.

Muttering and cursing, Marta pulled her sturdiest boots onto her feet and wrapped her cloak around her shoulders. I'll show the old hag, she thought. I'll bring her violets and shove them right in her face.

The fire snapped on, unperturbed, as Marta slammed out the door again.

Piles of snow, blown into unworldly shapes by the wind, covered the path that Marta would have taken through the forest had it been summer. No matter, she knew others. She spent as much time as possible in the wood when the weather allowed, and sometimes even when it didn't. Anything to get away from those two cows at home. Misha was boring and Mama was, well, Mama was everything bad rolled into one.

Within the shelter of the trees the way became clear. Most of the snow was held high above the ground, caught in the thick branches where it glistened in the dull light of a sinking sun. Marta knew that she had a good few hours before supper would be served. Or, she could take as long as she liked, for she was the one who would serve that supper. Why not make them wait? Why not let them go hungry? It would serve them both right.

Marta was in good spirits. Cold it might be, but she would rather freeze to death than scrub those horrible pots and pans.

The path veered into an unknown part of the forest and Marta, on a whim, decided to follow it, though the frost had crept into her pores. The incline grew steep; her breath came heavy and misted the air in front of her face with pearly drops of dew. Trees that smelled of ages gone grew around her in thick columns, bark black above the few white clumps of snow that huddled in their roots.

She soon came upon a clearing, where the trees fanned out around a silent scene. She stopped. Before her ice-crusted eyes sat a sight stranger than any she had ever seen. A mighty fire blazed in the center of a circle of throne-shaped rocks and on each rock perched a beautiful woman, twelve women in all. Marta gaped, but relinquished her surprise in a heartbeat and made for the warmth of the flames.

A woman with hair that fell to her feet in drifts as

white as the snow turned towards Marta as she strode up to the fire.

"You might have asked to join us," she said with a voice that shocked the clearing. Above Marta's head a limb broke with a loud snap and she scrambled out of the way as it fell.

"Sister, don't be so harsh. The girl is cold," said another of the women.

"Hush," said yet another. "Someone around here has to show some manners."

Marta looked from one face to another. "You don't have to be so nasty," she said to the woman who had first spoken. Why didn't she seem cold? She had hardly any covering.

"What is your name, child?" the woman asked with icicles in her eyes.

"I am not a child." Marta stamped her foot, raising a small flurry of snow.

"Now who's being nasty," the white woman sneered. Her crown of icy spires glinted as she bent forward to peer into Marta's face. "Answer the question."

Marta tossed her head within its hood. "My name is Marta."

A golden woman on the other side of the circle leaned forward. She had hair of braided sunlight and a dress that shone with such brilliance that Marta had to squint when she looked her way.

"What brings you into our part of the forest?" Her voice dripped honey onto the frozen ground and, as Marta watched, the snow at her feet melted, revealing a sprig of green.

"My father's wife sent me out to find violets for the table." Marta's explanation was cut short by laughter that bounced around the circle, causing limbs above to rattle like chimes in a breeze.

"Violets!" said a woman whose russet hair was held back by a crown of dried leaves and thorns. "January, did you hear that?" she chuckled with mirth. "You'll have a hard time finding violets while January sits in the high seat."

Marta flung her gaze at the woman named January. She had thought of her as the old one, with her skin made of ice. Now that she looked more closely at the women, they all seemed to be of the same age.

"I'm going to find those violets, you just watch and see!" Marta shouted at January's chill facade.

"Oh, we'll watch, never fear. In fact, we'll even help you." January bared teeth that were shards of ice in her stark white face.

She rose from her seat and gestured to another sister, a grand woman whose gown hung in hundreds of shades of green that trailed over the ground, leaving patches of buttercups in her wake. "March, would you be so kind?"

"Certainly, my sister," said March, a coy glint in her blue eye. The other was gray, unfathomable, and it pierced through Marta's skull, seeing all that lurked within.

March planted herself on the high seat with a sigh. She felt that she would become one of the rocks if she sat on them much longer. She faintly hoped that they would get some sport out of this girl. As her knees bent, the landscape changed. The snow melted away into the earth and in its place grew a field of green, dotted all over with tiny, fresh violets.

"There are your violets, girl. Pick them quickly, I can't sit here much longer."

Marta grabbed a handful of the brilliant flowers, tucked them into her apron and ran off into the wood without a word. March laughed as she stood, returning January's throne.

"What was that?" she asked the circle.

October shrugged and a sleeve of burgundy satin slipped from her shoulder. "Some human trick, no doubt. Violets in this month! Who would have thought of such a thing?"

February tittered, the sound of ice cracking on a pond. "I don't know, but whoever it was has a wondrous imagination. Or a wicked one." Her sisters nodded in agreement.

"Well," said January, snow falling again as she sat, restored to her throne, "at least it broke the monotony, if only for a moment." January shuddered, secretly feeling that the surrounding trees had caged them all in, edging closer and closer as the years had passed, until all that was left was this tiny circle from which there was no escape.

May sighed eloquently. "Maybe she'll come back." A flower grew out of her mouth as she spoke and she plucked it, tossing it to the ground in disgust as the others laughed.

"You really need to learn to control yourself," said November.

"Oh, hush." May replied.

"Not even a word of thanks," October commented

with a shake of her head.

Marta's face bore a smirk the entire way home. This will show Mama, she thought to herself as she entered the kitchen quietly, intending to surprise.

Mama heard her from the parlor. "Take off your cloak, you'll soak the floor," she called.

Marta sneered in reply. "Oh, but I have something for you, your grace." Her eyes were hard as coal in her shining face. From her apron she pulled the violets, as fresh as they had been when she tore them from the ground.

Mama was astonished and angry, but refused to show Marta a thing. She took the violets from Marta's hand. "Our supper wants cooking," she said and turned away.

That evening, Misha marveled at the violets in the vase. How had Marta done it?

The following morning the violets were dead, dried to a crisp, their color muted; their delicate petals had fallen to the table. Mama smiled.

"Marta!"

"What now?" Marta, brushing the dust from her apron onto the floor, had expected this. "Didn't you get enough out of me yesterday with your precious violets?"

"Ah, Marta, the violets were not as fresh as they seemed. Look, they are already dead!" Mama smiled. "Misha and I have a craving for strawberries. No tricks! We want them fresh for our dinner."

"Go pick them yourself," said Marta, who did not relish another trek in the cold.

"But you are the only one who knows where to find them," Mama spoke, "and I have dresses to mend."

"Send Misha, then. I don't want to go." Misha glanced at Mama, desperate, quietly praying that she would heed Marta's advice. She so wanted to be free of the house and away from them.

"You know better than to argue with me, Marta." Mama was firm. "I'll take the broom to your backside. Go now!" Misha thought of her embroidery, the endless drudgery of needle and thread, and a tear slipped from her eye. She brushed it away, quick, before Mama saw it.

In a huff, Marta grabbed her cloak. She did not want a beating today, she told herself and besides, she knew just where to go. Those women had helped her yesterday; they would do so again today. She was sure of it.

Marta climbed the small mountain, making her way to the fire that burned at its peak. Nothing had changed; the women sat around it, unmoving until she entered their icy glade.

"I'm back," she announced.

"So we see." January smiled like a cat that had just seen a treat come within easy reach.

"Give me strawberries," said Marta. "The old woman wants strawberries today. The violets weren't good enough."

August, the woman made of burnished gold, spoke roughly. "What makes you think we'll give you anything more than we have?"

"You must!" cried Marta. "You helped yesterday, why not today?"

"Oh for heaven's sake, calm yourself, girl," said January. "What will you give us if we do?"

Marta grew angry. "Why should I give you any-thing? Besides, I have nothing to give."

"Tell us a story then," July said from behind a fiery veil of hair, her slim, brown fingers clinging tightly to the rock on which she perched.

"I don't know any stories."

"You must!" said April, smoothing the pleats of her shimmering dress with a languid hand. "Every-one knows at least one story. Tell us now." Her glance met June's green eyes. June laughed.

"Fine." Marta tapped her frozen lips with a finger and began. "Once upon a time there was an evil woman who made her stepdaughter do all of the work while her true-daughter did nothing but sit around all day sewing. One day the stepdaughter got mad and ran away and the others, unable to wash even the simplest pot, died from neglect. The end."

"Oh, very good!" clapped May, ripe jewels on her fingers glinting in the sunlight that splayed through the branches above.

"How droll," said December.

"You just don't want to be entertained." May was peeved by her sister's inability to enjoy whatever little games came their way. She knew it was true; she had been sitting here with her for ages. They were all trapped, with only each other for company. They should make the most of it as they could.

Marta watched for a moment as the sisters squab-bled amongst themselves. Her patience expired; she spoke. "I told you a tale, now give me the strawberries."

"My, my," said August, flinging her long hair over her shoulder. "What ever is the rush?"

"You aren't the best company," Marta replied with a nasty smile. "I want to get out of here."

"Well then," said January, "we had better hurry lest the queen chastise us yet more!" She beckoned to June, who rose from her stony seat and glided over to the high throne, her purple dress rustling around her ankles, leaving spirals in the snow.

As she sat, the snow again melted and tall grasses grew in its place. Among the stems Marta saw strawberries bloom and fatten. She reached down and plucked up a handful, roots and all.

As she ran back down the path, January waved goodbye. "We'll see her again, I'm sure of it," she said to her sisters.

"Oh good," said September. "I can hardly wait."

"Why is that child so ill-tempered?" asked May.

"Who knows? There's something to that story she told, I would guess." October twisted a snarl of her thick hair and pulled at the dark silk of her dress.

"Don't you get tired of playing with yourself?" asked July, who had long ago resigned herself to their dreadful routine.

"Doesn't that rock make your bottom ache?" cracked August in reply.

June shook her head. Would anything ever change? Her sisters were so tiresome. She was sure they all felt the same of her. There was really no hope for it, they were caught in time and the pattern of time and they always would be.

MARTA EMPTIED HER APRON onto the carving board as Mama watched with dismay the ripe, red berries roll over the pale wood.

"I suppose you are pleased with yourself," she said.

"And why shouldn't I be?" Marta gloated. "It isn't as though you went out into the cold to find your own fruit."

Mama tasted one of the berries and spat it out. "Sour!" she shouted. "I told you I wanted them fresh!"

"You get what you deserve," Marta said with glee.

Crack! Mama's hand connected with Marta's cheek. "Apples! Get back out there and get me ripe apples."

"Fine!" Marta shouted. "I hope they poison you!"

"You're the only poison around here." Mama hissed.

Misha, in the parlor, covered her ears with shaking hands. Would they ever stop?

"OH LOOK, IT'S MARTA AGAIN. What a surprise," August said as Marta approached the fire. "We won't bother to invite her, will we, sisters?" A ripple of laughter made its way around the circle.

"No," said November, "but we will expect to be asked for help." She shifted on her rock, her black skirts gleaming under a cold sun.

"What will it be this time?" January was already finding the game tiresome.

"Apples. She wants apples."

"How inventive!" April crowed, evincing a glare from Marta. April stuck her tongue out at the girl.

"But no tricks this time! I don't want to come back."

"Tricks?" asked September.

August giggled like a child. "Is our hospitality not to your liking?"

Marta glared at them both.

January, a mischievous smile on her face, stood, making way for September to take the throne.

September always did put on airs, June thought, watching as her autumnal sister perched with grace upon the rock. Wind whirled the snow into gleaming devils and as it melted, the air became tainted with the scent of mulch. Leaves grew, greened and then fell, brown and curled. There, hanging from the branches of a nearby tree, were ripe, red apples, just waiting for Marta's greedy hand.

September smiled in triumph. "There are your apples, young Marta. Enjoy them!"

"No tricks!" shouted Marta as she pulled one down.

"You may only have two of them, you insolent thing," January broke in.

"Only two? Why not more?"

"Because I said so." January drew herself up and towered over the glade. An icy wind blew and the apples began to fall, rotten and pulpy, from the tree.

"All right! Just two," Marta cried and took the last one allotted her.

"We'll see you next time!" called June.

"No, you won't!" Marta didn't care what her stepmother wanted. She was not coming back to this horrible place.

Mama's face turned to plum when she saw the dried apples that Marta pulled from her pouch.

"They're useless!"

"So are you!"

Misha, in the parlor, had finally had enough. She couldn't bear their words pounding into her ears, scattering her thoughts and shrieking through her silence. Maybe it kept them entertained, but she could take no more.

"I'll get some apples," she said, her words creating a quiet pool in the smoky kitchen.

Mama stared. "I forbid it."

Misha shook her head. "I'm going." She pulled her own heavy cloak about her shoulders and went through the door and into the wood, leaving Mama and Marta to banter and bicker in the stew of their mutual misery.

She followed in Marta's footsteps. The snow was tramped down into an easy path and though she had no idea where it would lead, she did not care. She was free, if only for a while.

Soon enough she came to a bend in the path and ahead could see the flickering light of a large fire. Undaunted, she traveled on until she came to the circle of women, perched on their stony seats. She was tired and the fire looked very inviting. She hoped to find some welcome there, for her cheeks hurt with the cold.

As she stepped from behind a tree, twelve glorious heads swung her way.

"Hello," Misha said. "May I warm myself at your fire?"

January blinked. This was not Marta. Where was Marta?

"Who are you?" she asked the young woman. "How did you find us?"

"I followed the path made by my sister. My name

is Misha." She curtsied, as she had been taught to do.

"Come closer, girl," said August. "Of course you can warm yourself by the fire."

December glared at her sister. Trying to play nice, was she? "What do you want?" December said, the sharp edge of her voice slicing neatly through any kindness August might have offered.

Misha was not bothered. "I don't want anything. I told them I was looking for apples, but I really just needed to get away." She shrugged.

"That bad, is it?" June inquired.

"Sometimes." Misha did not wish the share the details with strangers. She was happy enough to have found even a small amount of warmth. "That's a lovely dress," she said to June, awed by the flowers that seemed to grow out of its very fabric.

June preened. "Thank you!"

September rolled her eyes.

Misha smiled as she gazed around the circle. The sisters seemed nice, in their own way. "You're the months, aren't you?"

January sat up in her throne, straight as an ice-covered pine. "How very astute of you to notice." She was pleased and she saw that her sisters were, as well.

"I could tell by the way each of you sits. You," she pointed to the woman of gold, "you must be August. You slouch as though smitten by summer's heat. And you," she looked at June, "are upright — not as fresh as May, beside you, but still expectant."

June and August glanced at each other sharply while around them the sisters laughed at Misha's observations.

"But," Misha continued, "if I may ask, what is that you do here on the mountain?"

January frowned. Here was the heart of the problem. "We don't do anything. We sit, year after year, stuck on these awful rocks. When my time has passed, I will relinquish the high seat to February and when her time is done, March takes the throne. And so on. It never changes."

No wonder they seemed on edge. Misha knew all about boredom and borders, she had plenty of both as she sat at her embroidery, day after long day, unable even to step out the door. She could not imagine centuries of it. Was there nothing they could do? Then it came to her — even though they must stay in their grotto, they weren't fixed to their seats.

"Why don't you trade thrones at random?" she asked.

"Impossible!" December rose from her seat and then, somewhat flustered, flounced back down upon the stone.

"Can't be done," May intoned.

"What are you suggesting?" January had an odd gleam in her eye.

"Well," Misha began, "January could try sitting for April and February could try sitting for March. That sort of thing."

January's brows spiked up. "Do you think we could?"

"I don't see why not. It would almost be like a game of dress-up. When I was young I used to try on all of my mother's clothes and jewels and pretend I was someone else for a day."

"We shouldn't!" April cried, and the others echoed her.

January's eyes flashed and the forest around them cracked under its skin of ice. "Why shouldn't we?"

"You do so much for others, but what does anyone do for you?" Misha looked at the months in turn, hoping they would at least consider her suggestion.

The sisters tittered, whispering behind their hands, leaning into each other and eyeing Misha as though she had dumped a pail of water on their fire. How could she suggest such a thing and, could it work? They sensed a change come over them, they felt the ring of trees that caged them in fall back.

August spoke first. "I'd like to give it a try."

"I think I would, too," June agreed. "What say you, sisters?"

A flurry of conversation ensued — at last, something might change on the mountain.

"I think I'll be going now," Misha broke in. "Thank you for sharing your fire."

If the sisters agreed, Misha knew that she would have caused more mischief than even that brat Marta could have managed. Much more. She should feel bad for that, but she didn't. Instead, she felt badly for herself, and for the sisters, for they were all in the same situation.

"Thank you!" the sisters chorused.

As Misha walked off down the mountain, January shook her head in amazement. "She didn't ask for a single thing and look at what she's given us."

"We should give her something in return," April spoke.

"I know just what to do." The smile on January's face chilled even the warm heart of August.

Misha followed the path down the mountain, so lost in thought that she hardly noticed the green grasses poking up from beneath rotted leaves or the buds blooming on the trees above her head. It was not until the sweat began to gather on her temples that she bothered to look around at the forest through which she traveled.

She paused. Had spring come while she wandered in the wood? Had she been with the sisters so long?

The house sat in solitude as always. The small herb garden sprawled out from behind the kitchens in a tangle of green leaves and the trees in the nearby orchard were laden with budding fruit. The fence was the same as ever — but no, it leaned as though the spring mending had been missed.

Misha crept through the herbs, unruly and shot through with weeds, to unlatch the door to the kitchen. She expected to see Marta bent over the hearth but instead was greeted with silence and cobwebs in the corners. A note was held on the table beneath the weight of a large rock shaped strangely like a throne. She picked up the brittle paper.

"Misha," it read. "It has been many months since you went looking for apples. Your sister, Marta, has run away and I can wait for you no longer. I have gone into the city to stay with my sister. Though I have no hope of it, should you return, the house is yours, as I have no use for it now. Love, Mama."

The paper fell from her hand. Misha heard it whisper as it hit the cobbles in the floor and thought,

I'm sorry, Mama. And then she thought of Mama's cruel tricks on Marta and of how she'd allowed Misha nothing but needlepoint to fill her days. *Why should I be sorry?* She hung her cloak on its hook as a wide smile broke over her face, like the sun peeking through a clouded sky. She stepped into the parlor and grabbed up the hated embroidery, still on the table where she had left it. In the kitchen she started a fire and when it was crackling nicely, she tossed the thing, hoop and all, into the flames. Next she turned to the pump and filled a bucket with water, happily splashing her hands in a mountain of suds and slime as she washed the neglected pots.

As time passed, if the seasons seemed a little off kilter, with May being as chill as February had once been and January feeling more like October, Misha could only laugh. Though they played their games ceaselessly and caused no amount of mischief for the farmers of the land, they blessed Misha's gardens with fruit and herbs enough to keep her well stocked for all the seasons of her life. Though Misha had enjoyed her visit with the sisters and was ever grateful for the gift of freedom they had given her, she never did wander up the mountain path again. She preferred, instead, to remember the warmth of their fire and the smiles on the sisters' faces when they realized that their own trap had been sprung.

Vandana Singh
The Choices of Leaves

There is a cacophony of crows
Outside in the early dusk.
They flap urgently from skeletal
Tree to tree. Some leaves
Of red and gold still flutter
In the gaunt wood. Can the leaves hear
What the crows say? What stirs
In their dessicated veins, makes them
Dance in the still air?
The madness of crows is in the speech
They write on the sky. But what of leaves
Yet on the tree?

Perhaps
Their reds and golds
Flame to ash, rise in the air
Stretch wing, bellow raucously
At the world beyond the wood.

But there are some who sigh and drop.
Browning in their thousands on the ground
Crisp as cornflakes.

What will it be, oh leaf?
Oblivion or insanity?
Silence or speech?
Choose.
Choose.
Choose.

Larry Hammer

Pygmalion's Marriage

  Pygmalion of Cyprus was a sculptor
who found the local women lacked a full
appreciation of his work, and him.
They were as bad as critics — worse, at times.
For all he tried, they'd not return his calls
for second dates (the brush-off protocol),
or if they did, slept with others too
(his so-called friends), came to his studio
to bother him, and every single one'd
completely misread what his pieces meant —
except that girl who broke it off. And so
he carved himself a woman of his own.

  Desire formed his work: ideals and dreams
controlled his shaping hands until it seemed
in that sustained white heat she carved herself.
At last it finished, leaving his empty shell
to vegidaze upon his couch for days —
both effort and effect of formal grace.

  His artistry could not, here, be denied.
Her stone: rose-tinted white — in firelight,
soft flesh. Face: Aphrodite's, with small flaws —
a mortal beauty. Eyes: cast down; arms: poised
to cover breast and thigh — awareness that
allured. Perfection: but for one defect —
no life. Even there, he learned he could
deceive himself — for when they kissed,

didn't her hard lips flutter back? and when
he cupped her breast, didn't her warm stone strain
to meet his hand? Didn't she snuggle near?
But then she froze, exactly as before.
The more time spent with her — caressing, petting,
dressing her up in clothes and jewels and hats
and then undressing her for bed at night —
the more she teased him with her hints of life.
He couldn't sleep. He didn't leave his flat
except to get her gifts. He ate from cans.
Each day to night to dusk became a blur
of love, of loving her, a fervid lover,
till he convinced himself in love-lorn blear
that helpful Aphrodite'd hear his prayer.

Her festival — nine Cypriotic days
of wine, orgiastic rites, and wild parades —
had just begun. He gathered offerings
and walked through streets of torch-lit reveling
to where the temples danced about the square
with naked sacred prostitutes, ignored
by him. Before the altar and its flame,
as incense sent around soft coils of gray
he knelt and spilled the blood of doves for Her
and gave the Lady Love a stammered prayer:
"Give me a woman like my marble art."
For moments, endless moments, all he heard
was priestess/priest's eternal sex, and hymns —
then sacred fires rose and fell three times
in omen: Yes. Heart leaping lightning-like,
he hurried home to meet his new-made wife.

But when he thundered in, she lay (a lie)
in bed still stony unalive. He sighed
at — wait, — was that? — beneath his warming hand
her breast softened like beeswax till it handled
as fleshly firm as any maidens' should.
He stroked her yielding thigh, felt her flesh's blood,
and kissed her mouth, which parted to his tongue.
She breathed, a slender shudder of newborn lung,
then Galatea opened her eyes to see
Pygmalion look down. Enraptured, he
caressed her to convince himself it was true,
and she replied as instinct told her to:
with joy at painless birth, and legs apart.
He moved between them and with lover's art
they consummated what great Aphrodite granted.

As always after pausing, time recanted
and hauled the lovers from their hungry bed:
soon people heard Pygmalion was wed —
to everyone's surprise — and came to see.
His friends mistook her, understandably,
for her model, and praised how accurate
his details were — for they saw every bit,
at least till Galatea learned to dress:
created nude, she simply couldn't guess
why clothing must be worn, and anyway
her clothes were all ill-fitting lingerie.
But he bought better suits that weren't so raw
and Modesty (bastard child of Sex and Law)
was learned — along with life's essential skills:
to cook and clean, chat up the imbeciles
at galleries, and understand his art.

These came as fillies walk — the flirting part,
at least, for socially, she soon matured.
(His consolation: several sales she lured.)
But as for taste, that seemed a hopeless quest:
she thought his early hackwork was his best.

   At least the sex was great — till it became
the fuel, not damper, of their quarrel's flames
for, shaped as sexiness incarnate, and
woken to sex, and watching festive bands
have constant sex her first eight days of life,
and loving sex, she just didn't get *why*
sex stopped. "A man can only pump," he said,
"till he runs dry." And putting it off? — that's mad.
"I have to work sometimes, to make a living."
And other men were always willing to give.
"You weren't carved for other —" And you know,
those temple whores continuously screw.
"You're my wife, not a sacred prostitute —"
Oh yeah? "Yes —" We'll see about that, she shouted
and slammed shut the heavy metal door.
He stared at where she'd stood, now empty air.

   She stayed away two days. Pygmalion,
determined not to let that . . . trollop win,
did nothing but listen for her quiet step,
glance out the window, gnaw his lower lip,
again glance, take up chisel with a will
and not remember what he's doing, wilt,
begin to clean the flat — then stop in anger:
his own creation, his!, was in the wrong —
he'd not apologize by doing dishes.

The third day, confident, despite his rush,
she wasn't there, he walked with hurried steps
back to the temple. See? Not here — just men
watching a naked whore dance for the crowd.
"Who'd celebrate the love," the priestess called,
"our Mother gave Adonis once? Who'd give
our harvest all the strength of her and him?"
He recognized the body she displayed,
the one from which he'd chipped white stone away,
and stared, then pushed through the hindering
    throng
empty with fear and sense of fate and longing
too late to claim her — a merchant tithed
his offering and guided her inside.

He stood alone within the crowd: He'd seen
Galatea's smile — not his, her own.

Divorce was quick — the temple intervened:
conceived by mortal hand but born by Love,
she was the ideal vestal for their goddess;
she later rose to lead the cult, high priestess.
With therapy, Pygmalion grew calm
and gained success recarving her in small
for sale as idols in the temple shops
as aids for luck in love, and better crops.

Bud Webster

Of the Driving Away of a Certain Water Monster by the Virtue of the Prayers of the Holy Man
or
What *Really* Happened at Loch Ness in the Summer of 565 A.D.

THE RECENT DISCOVERY and publication of the diaries of the Wandering Jew (who, as it turns out, is neither much of a wanderer nor a Jew, but that's another story) has either shed remarkable light on — or cast a great shadow over — a great many subjects, depending on how much credence one gives them. The revelations concerning the true origins of the works of Shakespeare (from Vol. XXI, page 117: "He wrote them. I was there. Trust me."), the explosion over Tunguska in 1918, and the source of Da Vinci's ideas have fed academic and scientific controversy for the past decade.

As you will no doubt recall, immediately after publication the (non-)Wandering (non-)Jew released a statement to the world press through her lawyers indicating that a) no claims of veracity were made or implied, b) no discussion, verification, or confirmation of statements in the diaries would be forthcoming, and c) she wasn't making dime one off of this, since the diaries were indisputably in the public domain (the current copyright limitation — life of the author plus 75 years — does not apply to individuals born Before Christ).

For the purposes of this essay, I'll confine myself to the portions of the diaries relating to the now-legendary first sighting of the Loch Ness Monster.

There are, as you might imagine, a number of points of incongruity between the so-called historical record and the diaries, not the least of which is the accepted fact that there was no castle on that spot on the Loch until 1125, when a timbered earthwork was constructed on what was to become Urquhart Point, off Urquhart Bay. There were, in fact, no towers until 170 years later when Edward I of England installed Sir William Fitzwarine as keeper (himself replaced a year later by Sir Alexander Forbes, who gave the castle its present name).

When I noted this discrepancy in a letter sent to the alleged originator of the diaries through the above-mentioned law firm, the only reply I received was a rather cryptic note saying "Vas *you* dere, Cholly?" This obscure allusion refers to Bert Gordon, a radio comedian of the thirties for whom the above acted as a catch-phrase. The handwriting on the note has been verified by several experts as the same hand that wrote the diaries; make of that what you will. (In point of fact, any and all decisions about the possible verisimilitude of this account are left entirely to the reader.)

At the beginning of this conflict of legend versus "fact", there is St. Columba. Perhaps best known for bringing Christianity to Scotland, he is also credited with having chased the Monster of Loch Ness away solely by the power of the cross and the invocation of God's name.

Nothing, according to the diaries, could be further from the truth.

There is nothing in them that disputes his role in bringing Christianity to the "province of the Picts", and it is made quite clear that he "drove away" the Monster, albeit not in the way that St. Adamnan wrote in his famous biography of Columba (here quoted from the Carruth translation). However, Adamnan can be forgiven his exaggerations, if for no other reasons than his natural loyalty and enthusiasm.

Here's what St. Adamnan wrote about his fellow abbot:

[1] He found it necessary to cross the water Ness; and when he came to the bank thereof, he sees some of the inhabitants burying a poor unfortunate man, whom, as those who were burying him themselves reported, some water Monster had, a little before, snatched at him while he was swimming and bitten with a most savage bite, and whose hapless corpse some men who came in a boat to give assistance, though too late, caught hold of it by putting out hooks.

(We can, by exercising only a little magnanimity, also forgive St. Adamnan his apparent unfamiliarity

[1] Book 2, Chapter 27 of *The Latin Life of the Great St. Columba*, written by St. Adamnan, and translated by Father J. A. Carruth, O.S.B., in his *Loch Ness and Its Monsters*, Fort Augustus, Scotland: The Abbey Press, first edition, 1954.

with standards of punctuation, Strunk and White being some 1400 years in his future.)

Now, while it's quite true that St. Columba crossed from one side of the loch to the other, the diaries give another reason why:

[2] JUNE 16, IN THE YEAR OF OUR LORD 565. This day, a Monster arose from the loch, making a great splashing and noise in the Bay. The Monster lashed its tail against the walls of the redoubt, and the stones trembled at its onslaught, and the soldiers were afraid.

The locals employed at Castle Urquhart fell to their knees and prayed, but to no avail. The soldiers sent bolts and arrows at the Great Beast, threw Greek Fire and spears at it, but it did them no good. At last, the Lord of the castle himself ordered that the Abbot of the Benedictines at the other side of the loch be brought, to do what he could.

What do we know about this Abbot? He is said to have come from Ireland, and St. Adamnan describes him as "holy and famous", but the diaries indicate that, although having come to Iona *from* Ireland, Columba was originally from what later became Leeds in West Yorkshire. He was a big man, the son

---

[2] *The Early Diaries of the Wandering Jew, and Some Speculations on the "Truths" They Contain*, translated by Fra. Perelman, S.J., New York: Cardiff Press, in thirty-nine volumes, first (?) edition, 1990.

of a farmer, with black hair, a barrel chest, and hairy hands, and his manner was gruff and earthy, as befit a farmer's son.

Adamnan next says:

> The blessed man, however, on hearing this, directs that some of his companions shall swim out and bring to him the boat that is on the other side, sailing it across. On hearing this direction of the holy and famous man, Lugne Mocumin, obeying without delay, throws off all clothes except his undergarment, and casts himself into the water.

(Perhaps a foolish thing to do, but presumably the risk might seem considerably lessened when one is protected by a "holy and famous" companion.)

The diaries differ greatly on the above point:

> When the Abbot answered the summons, he was vexed at this interruption of his studies and meditations. "What's all this bloody foofaraw?" he asked the messenger, waving a stack of vellum sheets in the air. "I've got sixty bloody pages to get through before compline, and there's carrots to get in yet." The messenger described the Monster with great vehemence and fervor. "Oh, aye, all reet," the Abbot muttered. "But I conner get there on foot, tha' knows. Bring me yon coracle." And with the pages still in his hand, he stamped impatiently to the shore.

The most pronounced discrepancy in the two accounts occurs next. Adamnan's description doesn't include the castle at all; the diaries imply the castle was essential to the outcome.

Adamnan:

Now the Monster, which was not so much satiated as made eager for prey, was lying hid in the bottom of the river, but perceiving that the water above was disturbed by him who was crossing, suddenly emerged, and swimming to the man as he was crossing, rushed up at him with a great roar and open mouth.

And the diaries:

There was no clear sight of the creature, as a mist lay across the water. When the small boat touched the shore, the Abbot stepped briskly from it to the land and strode to the castle. As he came closer, the bay and its Visitor became visible to him, and he stopped and exclaimed "Bloody Hell!", shook his head, and walked on, muttering under his breath.

Adamnan:

Then . . . with his holy hand raised on high he did form the sign of the cross in the empty air, invoked the name of God, and commanded the fierce Monster, crying "Think not to go further nor touch thou that man. Quick! Go back!" Then the beast on hearing this voice of the saint, was terrified and fled backwards more rapidly than he had come, as if dragged by cords, although it had come so close to Lugne as he swam that there was not more than the length of a punt pole between the man and the Monster.

The diaries:

The Abbot kicked at the door of the castle, shouting to be let in. "Coom on, open 't door! I haven't got all bloody day!" The door was opened by a quaking servant, and the Abbot shook him by the scruff of the neck and cried "Take me to the top of yon tower, or I'll gi' ye one up the conk."

He was shown the way to the tower, as the stones shook and trembled at the Monster's assault, and water splashed in at even the highest windows. Several times the Abbot stumbled and almost fell, which didn't improve his temper.

Upon reaching the top of the tower, he leaned over the battlements and shouted, "Ey-up! You!" at the Monster, who, looking up at the sound, raised Its head as if to swallow him whole. But when Its head came even with the battlements, the Abbot rolled up the vellum sheets he had brought with him and struck the Beast a great blow across the snout. "Bad doggie! *BAD* doggie!" he cried, shaking his other fist in Its face. "Four o'clock on a Soonday, you make this bloody row? Be off, and don't coom back, or I'll take a stick to you!" And the Monster, whining piteously and with a look of great hurt on Its face, slunk back into the water and was not seen again, except once in a while when It thought the Abbot wasn't around. The Abbot himself stomped back down the stairs and out of the castle to the waiting coracle, pausing only to shake his head and mutter, "Manky Scots and their bloody animals."

So, what are we to make of all this? I'm sure there are those who will say that the preceding excerpt is not only inaccurate, but a scandalous pack of lies as well. There will be those for whom the diaries and their "revelations" are anathema, a slap in the face of reality. Others might nod sagely in seeming acceptance of the insights offered, but precious few of the history books will be re-written, I'm afraid.

Be that as it may, and in spite of the historical inaccuracies inherent in almost every line of the diaries, I find this account of the "Driving Away" eminently more satisfactory than the "original" version.

And to those who would dismiss their veracity, I would simply reply, "Vas *you* dere, Cholly?"

Theodora Goss
Goblin Song

In the bright May-time
When green herbs are springing,
Our hearts they are ringing
Like bells in a tower.

We dance as do maidens
Upon the cropped hillside
When wedding the bride
Unto chivalry's flower,

We prance as do fawnlets
All lissome and amber
And plash in the river
And play by its side,

We sway like the willows
That spring by the water
Or maidens with laughter
Saluting the bride.

Out, creepings, out, crawlings,
Come into the May-light
From out of your night
Underneath the high hill,

Come dance on the grasses,
Like maidens, like fawnlets,
Disporting grotesques
Celebrating our fill,

With knob-knees and horn-nubs,
Pug-noses and tails,
With moss-covered nails,
We crouch and we cower,

In the bright May-time
When green herbs are springing
And our hearts are ringing
Like bells in a tower.

Richard Parks
The Last Romantic

APRIL 17

D RAGONS MAKE MISTAKES. Especially when the
sun's out for the first time in ages and they can't
remember the last time they've been warm. I crawled
out of the cave and onto the rocks.

The kids almost saw me.

I scuttled back in, sent some pebbles rattling, but
luckily no harm done. It was a human boy and girl
and the only thing they were paying any attention to
was each other. I'd been a dragon so long that I'd
forgotten what life was like for others, so I watched
them. That was another mistake.

They brought a basket lunch and an old yellow
blanket, and the boy was scared and the girl was shy
and they fumbled with each other so sweetly that I
wanted to cry. I tried to imagine what it would be like
for the Princess and me on a picnic like that, with
furtive glances and tentative touchings, but such
things don't happen to dragons.

APRIL 18

Read over what I wrote yesterday. It sounds rather
bitter. I'm not, really. Say in all fairness that I didn't
understand my part from the beginning, but I learned
it soon enough, and besides, the knowledge didn't
change anything. When the sun is warm it brings back
the illusion of fresh starts and possibilities. That's why

I can write about what happened now.

I saw the Old Man last night.

The stars were out, but the darkness was solid enough for a dragon to hide in. I slipped down to the creek for a drink and there he was in the water just like a reflection, sitting in that creaking ladder-back chair like the first time. He opened his cracked-leather face and said, "I'll show you where to find something." That started me thinking and then remembering. Who I was, I mean. Had a name and everything. It was . . . damn, gone again. But the rest is still there and if it's still there tomorrow I'll write it down. I won't believe a word of it then, but that's all right — it passes the time.

APRIL 19

I still remember — I wasn't always a dragon. Once I drove a Ford and worked with other people who weren't dragons, and when you're not a dragon you have to find ways to amuse yourself. I hunted arrowheads in the north Alabama hills. I never disturbed archeological sites or burials or anything like that; I was no pot-hunter. I just wandered farmland, mostly with the owners' permission, seeing what the plows had turned up. I liked holding things other people had made long ago; it made the past real in a way history books never managed. It's the nature of romantics to search for belief outside themselves, and that requires symbols. We're probably responsible for a lot of religions.

So one day in late summer I drove my Ford into the hills and stopped at a little one-pump grocery to ask the locals about good sites. Inside it was cool and shadowy; the floor was covered with rough oak boards that creaked at every step like arthritic rats.

The old man sat at the only window, but he was looking at me with bright blue eyes that should have belonged to a much younger fellow. He scared me, you want the truth; I didn't know why then, but somehow I must have sensed what he was. There were three lance points lying on the window sill and they were beautiful! I had to ask about them; couldn't help myself. Walked right up to the old dragon and said "Hi! My name is . . . "

Crap.

Thought I could tease it past those dead gray cells, but no joy. Doesn't matter what I said then. *He* said "I'll show you where to find something." And he told me exactly how to get here. He wasn't at the store when I went back to kill him, to make the Princess mine alone. Not that I needed to, I realize now. He'd already crawled off somewhere to die alone. That's what dragons do when they're too old and sick to be dragons any longer.

So here I am now, looking at the Princess as I write this. She's lying in the back of the cave on a stone bed covered with bearskin, just like when I found her. I know "princess" isn't the right word, but I don't know a better one. She might be Cherokee but it's hard to say; I'm no expert. She has a band of copper around black hair that reaches her knees, cinnamon skin, a doeskin shawl covering dainty breasts, and her skirt and boots are beaded with porcupine quills. Sleeping Beauty, only this time I'm not reading the story. I'm in it.

It took me a long time to understand that difference. When you read the story you're always the hero or heroine. When you're *in* the story . . . well, someone else is in charge of casting. You might not be the hero.

You might be the dragon.

Oh, I tried to be the hero, believe me. I fought, clawed, crawled on my knees like a whimpering dog as I tried to reach the Princess. It was no use; something pushed me away. Gently, almost kindly. But firmly. The Princess is waiting, yes, but not for me.

Some men will try to destroy what they can't possess, but not true romantics. Not the real hopeless cases, anyway. The old dragon knew me the moment he saw me. Takes one to know one, as they say. The Old Man didn't want to stop being her dragon, but he was all used up. He had to stop. Just as I had to become her dragon in turn because there was nothing else I *could* do.

I've been a good dragon, I think. Oh, sure, I take some risks, slipping into town now and then to steal writing supplies; talking to myself on paper helps me keep what passes for sanity. But I've never shirked my duties: I've kept her safe, and I've learned all the things good dragons know — how to make the mouth of a cave look like blank rock, how to keep people away, how to live on nearly nothing. It's all part of the plan.

All right, so I don't know the plan. I'm just going on faith here. I believe there is one. I'll think about it later. Right now I'm going to gaze at my Love for a while.

APRIL 22

Should have known better. There's nothing more pathetic than a Romantic trying to reason any pattern out of whole cloth. It's all gut and gland, instinct and emotion with us. But I do have a feeling, summed thusly — Arthur and his knights may indeed be sleeping under the hills of Avalon and there just might be one glorious, liberating battle at the end of it all, but, if the fates *really* wanted to shake things up, the only one coming out of that hill would be Guenivere. You want to win a war, don't give people someone to fight for them. Give them something to fight for.

When I think of what has happened to the Princess's people for the last few hundred years, I can see the parallels even clearer. The Great White Father in Washington will never know what hit him.

As I said, it's just a feeling, a notion. I don't know if it's true or not. Whatever magic is working here, understanding on my part doesn't seem to be required. That's all right; I know my place now. Still, I would like to think there's a point to this, other than my compulsion and nature forcing me to do what I had to do.

APRIL 23

Thought I saw the old dragon in the water again today, but I was wrong. It was me. When did I get so old?

APRIL 24

First the old dragon, now the others. They flit

among the trees by the creek, hide behind limestone boulders on the hillside. They watch me from shadows like starving wolves around a campfire. They are the shadows. I know who they are. Ghosts.

Let them try, if they dare. She's still mine. It's still my turn, and theirs is long past. I won't give her up to them or anyone without a fight. I am the dragon.

APRIL 26

Two days but they come no closer. They're waiting for something. I feel it, too. Someone is coming. The new dragon? Yes, it must be. I try to think how I'll test him. The old dragon was gentle, but I can't be with this new one. He'll have to prove himself to me in the only way he can. I feel like a campfire in that last bright flare before the logs fall to ashes and the wind takes all. I may look human but I know what I am within this husk — I stretch my wings against the sun.

Let him come now.

MAY 1

He heard me; I know it. He's coming. The ghosts of the other dragons draw back a little, but I see them clearer than ever. There's little of the dragon left in them now: wing stumps on hunched backs, broken claws, flickering eyes. The rest is human — tired, beaten old men. But they remember her, remember what it was like to be dragons, and the fire is still in their eyes. Death is no release for us; I know that now.

Soon I will join them.

I was wrong. It isn't the new dragon.

He's chanting again — the hero's calling me. *Uktena*. I don't understand the word, but I know what it means. It's a name. It's what the hero thinks I am. When I drop my guard a bit I can see the shape he's trying to force on me — the granddaddy of all serpents, with a head the color of polished rubies, the horns of a deer, and a spiked crest of rock crystal. It's what he expects me to be, the terrible beast between him and the Princess. Lovely image and very flattering, but I force the vision away and cling to my own form. I'm not an *uktena*, I'm a dragon. I've earned my name. I'll keep it.

I can only imagine what the hero went through to get here. Did he grow up with the remnants of the old traditions, perhaps supplementing what remained with books? Lured with the Old Stories, perhaps? Dreams? Maybe there was someone on their side to point him to me at the proper time, as the old dragon led me to the Princess. I imagine there was.

What else? He'll be young, of course. Handsome. Everything the Princess needs. Everything that I am not. I picture dark eyes, dark hair. Which will be worn traditionally long, of course, and he'll have a feather stuck in it somewhere. Eagle, if he can get it. A beaded necklace, faded jeans. Old and new together.

He's afraid, and I don't blame him for that.

There's Power in that chant; the human husk crumbles away and the pale flesh turns to dust. I thought it would hurt to surrender the last of my humanity; I was prepared for the sacrifice but I expected pain. There is no pain. It feels wonderful as I'm revealed at last: Iridescent scales, majestic wings . . . I'm beautiful!

One last look at my Beloved and then out into the sunlight. It'll be a glorious fight and I will do my best because the Princess deserves no less, but I don't think I can win. I don't want to — that would spoil everything. Poor hero, there's really nothing to fear from me. He can't know that, of course. He has to be afraid, and try anyway. Otherwise he wouldn't be the hero.

Odd . . . I didn't think there would be any regrets, but there is one — the Princess will never know I loved her, or how magnificent I was for her on this final day. I won't be so magnificent when he's done with me.

Damn.

Could that be it?

It's hard to write — claws — but I have to get it down. I have to tell someone how the story ends . . . how I think it ends. The magic ends with me; the Princess will wake to the hero's touch. She will love him and be with him; they will fight their battles together and, perhaps, grow old and die together. But for us, dragons, for *us* she remained young and eternal and yes, very beautiful. And that's something she'll never do for *him*.

Is that love, I wonder? Maybe just a little?

Probably not.

But for romantic fools and dragons it will have to do.

Theodora Goss
Beauty to the Beast

When I dare walk in fields, barefoot and tender,
Trace thorns with my finger, swallow amber,
Crawl into the badger's chamber, comb
Lightning's loose hair in a crashing storm,
Walk in a wolf's eye, lie
Naked on granite, ignore
The curse on the castle door,
Drive a tooth into the boar's hide,
Ride adders, tangle the horned horse,
When I dare watch the east
With unprotected eyes,
Then I dare love you, Beast.

Joe Haldeman
god is dead short live god

for Lester del Rey

they hold no sway over us
whose names were never written down
but only mumbled in fear and reverence
the ur-gods   forgotten when their last believer died
their crude avatars dusty lumps
in museum drawers
> *This fat "madonna" was a god of fertility;*
> *note the exaggerated vagina and breasts. This one*
> *must*
> *have been death, with its Halloween grin and*
> *empty ribcage.*

jupiter died   and ares and demeter and pan
and loki and quetzalcoatl and bacchus
when the last splash of wine or blood dried on their
    altars
and the last human who loved or hated or feared
    them
no longer could make it to church   they died
who only lived while we believed

and so will go moses jehovah jesus mohammed
when the last reverent brain is bashed out
by someone who believes otherwise
or when their followers' unprotected souls

dissipate in radioactivity
delivered by infidels
fearing neither hell nor heaven

how short might be a reign of science
how long could its gleaming altar   technology
demand belief   instill reverence   conjure mystery
and what sweet god will replace it

About the Authors

Mike Allen's previous projects as an editor of fiction and /or poetry include *New Dominions: Fantasy Stories by Virginia Writers* ('95), the webzine *Event Horizon* ('96 to '98), and the poetry magazine *Mythic Delirium* ('98 to now). Most recently, he co-edited *The Alchemy of Stars: Rhysling Award Winners Showcase*, which collects the Rhysling Award-winning poems from 1978 to 2004 in one volume. He lives in Roanoke, Va., with his wife Anita, two comical dogs and a demonic cat. His website is www.descentintolight.com.

Matthew Cheney has published fiction and nonfiction in a variety of places, including *Strange Horizons*, *Failbetter.com*, *Locus*, *Rain Taxi*, *Pindeldyboz*, and *Rabid Transit: Menagerie*. His website is http://mumpsimus.blogspot.com.

Constance Cooper has worked as an editor, balloon twister, linguistic researcher, and software engineer. She holds degrees in journalism and linguistics, and currently lives in the San Francisco Bay Area with her husband and baby daughter. Her website is at http://constance.bierner.org.

Gary Every lives and works in Sedona, Arizona. His poems have appeared in *Dreams and Nightmares*, *Hadrosaur Tales*, *Mythic Delirium* and other places. His novella, *Inca Butterflies*, is available from Hadrosaur Productions.

Theodora Goss has been writing poetry since she can remember. Her poems have been published in magazines such as *Mythic Delirium* and *The Lyric*, and reprinted in *The Year's Best Fantasy and Horror*. She recently won a Rhysling Award. Her chapbook of short stories and poems, *The Rose in Twelve Petals & Other Stories*, was published by Small Beer Press, and a short story collection, *In the Forest of Forgetting*, is currently available from Prime Books. She lives in Boston, where she is completing a PhD in English literature, with her husband, daughter, and cats. Her website address is www.theodorgoss.com. ("Beauty to the Beast" first appeared in *The Lyric*, Summer 1993.)

Joe Haldeman's latest books include the James Tiptree Jr. Award-winning *Camouflage*, the novel *Old Twentieth* and the collection *War Stories*, containing all his writings about the Vietnam War. His many honors include five Hugos, four Nebulas, the World Fantasy Award and three Rhysling Awards for poetry. His rhymed double sestina "Old Twentieth (A Century Full of Years)" received a standing ovation when he read it at the first-ever public ceremony for presentation of the Rhysling Awards in 2005.

Larry Hammer's most recent poems and stories have apeared in *The First Heroes*, *Abyss & Apex*, and *Say . . . have you heard this one?*. He lives in Arizona with his wife, Janni Lee Simner.

Richard Parks is a native of Mississippi, where he lives with his wife and three cats. PS Publishing will bring out his novella, *Hereafter and After*, as a signed limited edition in late 2006. His second story collection, *Worshiping Small Gods*, is due out from Prime Books in June 2006.

Charles Saplak has published fiction and poetry in numerous magazines and anthologies. When not writing he likes gardening and woodworking. He can be reached at saplak@verizon.net. ("Cemetery Seven" first appeared in *Terminal Fright*, Nov./Dec. 1993.)

Vandana Singh writes speculative fiction and teaches college physics. Her short stories have been published in numerous venues, including *Polyphony*, *Trampoline*, *The Third Alternative* and *Strange Horizons*, as well as a couple of *Year's Best* anthologies. Her first book for children, *Younguncle Comes to Town*, originally published in India, debuts in the U.S. on April 6, 2006 from Viking Children's Books.

Lawrence Schimel is a full-time author, anthologist, and translator who has published over 70 books, including *The Drag Queen of Elfland*, *His Tongue*, *Two Boys in Love*, *Things Invisible to See: Lesbian and Gay Tales of Magic Realism*, *Camelot Fantastic*, *Tarot Fantastic*, and others. His poem "How to Make a Human" won a Rhysling Award, his anthology *PoMoSexuals* won a Lambda Literary Award, and his picture book *No Hay Nada Como El Original* (with illustrations by Sara Rojo Pérez) was selected by the International Youth Library in Munich for the White Ravens. He lives in Madrid.

Sonya Taaffe has a confirmed addiction to myth, folklore, and dead languages. Her poem "Matlacihuatl's Gift" shared first place for the 2003 Rhysling Award, and a respectable amount of her short fiction and poetry were recently collected in *Postcards from the Province of Hyphens* and *Singing Innocence and Experience* (Prime Books). She is currently pursuing a Ph.D. in Classics at Yale University.

Catherynne M. Valente writes novels and poetry and occasionally deconstructs Greek plays for fun and profit. Her novels include *The Labyrinth*, *Yume no Hon: The Book of Dreams*, *The Grass-Cutting Sword* (all from Prime Books) and, forthcoming from Bantam/Dell in November, *The Orphan's Tales*. Her poetry books include *Apocrypha* and *Oracles*. Her website is http://www.catherynnemvalente.com/

JoSelle Vanderhooft is a Utah-based poet, novelist and freelance writer. Her books include *10,000 Several Doors*, *The Tale of the Miller's Daughter*, *Vice of Kings*, *Enter, Elsinore* and *Desert Songs* among others. Her poetry and short stories have appeared or will appear online and in print in *Star*Line*, *Cabinet des Fées*, *Sybil's Garage*, *Mythic Delirium*, *The Seventh Quarry* and others.

Ian Watson has been writing SF and fantasy for a long time, which is how he has produced about 30 novels and 10 story collections, not because he's prolific or writes fast. His most recent collection is *The Butterflies of Memory* (from PS Publishing in June 2006), and his most recent novel *Mockymen* (Golden Gryphon, 2003). 2001 saw the publication of his first poetry collection, *The Lexicographer's Love Song* (DNA Publications) and the screening of Steven Spielberg's *A.I. Artificial Intelligence*, for which Ian has screen credit for Screen Story, based on working for a year with Stanley Kubrick. His website is at www.ianwatson.info.

Bud Webster has twice won *Analog* magazine's Analytical Laboratory award, once for Best Short Story, and once for Best Novelette. His narrative SF hobo poem, "The Ballad of Kansas McGriff," took first place in the National Hobo Association's Music and Poetry Festival in 2000. He's also written non-fiction extensively, including essays in *The New York Review of Science Fiction*, and *The Magazine of Fantasy & Science Fiction*. He lives in Richmond, Virginia with a very patient Significant Other and three damn cats. ("Of the Driving Away . . . " first appeared in *A Distant Soil* #30 by Colleen Doran, Aug. 2000).

Erzebet YellowBoy's short stories have appeared in *Fantasy Magazine* and are forthcoming in *Jabberwocky 2*, *Not One of Us* and *Sleeping Beauty, Indeed*. She is the founder of Papaveria Press and co-editor of *Cabinet des Fées*, a journal of fairy tale fiction and in her spare time, she plays with bones.

Printed in the United Kingdom
by Lightning Source UK Ltd.
126966UK00001B/49/A